Praise

"I loved it :) Historically correct with glimpses into the lives of 4 women and they're small town as the civil war breaks out. Ms. LaPres, what an outstanding debut! You must read it, I promise you won't be disappointed."

"I totally enjoyed the writing of this first time author. It was clear, concise and factually accurate to the era. I would not hesitate to read another of her works!!"

"I love historical fiction and I felt that this book was well written and factual. I can't wait for the sequels to come out. Nice job for a first time author."

"I had trouble putting the book down. Couldn't wait to find out what was going to happen next. I look forward to reading more about the other characters."

"Well written and factual. Couldn't put it down. Looking forward to the next book."

"This is an awesome book to read. It got me so involved it was hard to put down. I can't wait to read the next one. I highly recommend this book."

"I just finished the book and thoroughly enjoyed it. You included so many elements in your book that are often overlooked with the "strategy" of war. Through the relationship of 4 amazing women (and one antagonist), you were able to discuss the personal relationships of friends, husbands, and families. You presented the struggles of these women and the prejudice that existed besides that of color. And you added the struggle of faith as well."

"Read your book. It was AWESOME! And I really mean it. Interesting characters, great plot, even had tears in my eyes a couple of times!"

Wherever You Go

A Turner Daughters Novella

Marie LaPres

This novel is dedicated to my wonderful and loving grandparents.

To the readers...

This is a historical fiction novel based in multiple cities in the years before the Civil War. Some characters are fiction, while other characters are based on actual historic figures that lived during the time period. Be sure to read the Authors Note at the end of the book to learn more about the characters.

"Don't urge me to leave you or to turn back from you. Where you go I will go, and where you stay I will stay. Your people will be my people and your God my God.

-Ruth 1:16

Part 1: 1857

Friday, June 26, 1857
Byron Hill Plantation
Outside Charleston, South Carolina

"Oh, I wish I was in the land of cotton, old times there are not forgotten..." Augusta Byron sang to herself as her maidservant, Emmy, finished putting her hair in an elegant chignon. She smiled at the reflection in the mirror. She saw her smooth blonde hair with sunshine highlights that hung almost to the small of her back when down, sparkling green eyes, and a figure that many women had expressed an envy of.

"I almost done, Miz Augusta," Emmy said.

"Very good," Augusta replied, leafing through her fans, deciding which one to take with her to the dinner and dance tonight. Her brother Joseph was coming home from the West Point Military Academy in New York today, and she couldn't wait to see him. It had been two years since she had last visited him, which was far too long, especially since she considered him to be one of her closest friends.

"Miz Augusta." Diane, Emmy's mother and Augusta's former nursemaid, poked her head in the room. "Miz Margaret here ta see ya."

"You can bring her right up." Augusta met Diane's eyes in the mirror. "Thank you, Diane." The slave nodded and hastened downstairs.

"I didn't know Miz Margaret was comin' fo dinner tonight." Emmy tucked one final strand into Augusta's chignon.

"Father told me I could invite her. You know that Margaret has been friends with the family for ever so long, it's as if she's part of the family. In fact, when we were up in New York visiting Joseph, he introduced her to his friends as 'like my sister'. I am positive he will be pleased to see her."

"I see. An' is Mista Joseph bringin' any of his friends home?"

"I don't know for sure. He has many acquaintances I believe, but only one true friend, from what I can gather from his letters."

'That be the cadet that wouldna even talk ta ya?"

"I don't believe it was a matter of not wanting to talk with me so much as it was that he couldn't speak to me." Augusta smiled at the thought of Joseph's friend, Michael Lewis. Tall and thin, with dark hair, and she had barely been able to notice that his eyes were brown, as he failed to meet her own eyes more than once or twice. "He was so shy, I declare it was almost painful."

"Maybe ya intimidated him."

"Perhaps," Augusta stood and adjusted her skirts.

"Will Mista Jeffrey be comin'?" Emmy asked.

"Not until the reception tomorrow," Augusta replied. "He had some business in Charleston to attend to." Jeffrey Cullen was her beau, and Joseph had yet to meet him. "I am anxious for him to meet Joseph. I believe they will get along splendidly."

"I hope so," Emmy replied as the door opened and Margaret Wiggs waltzed into the room. Margaret was considered one of the most beautiful women in the area, with midnight black hair and deep blue eyes. Many men would give their fortunes for the honor of marrying her, and she had broken many hearts. Unfortunately, Augusta suspected that her oldest brother, Andrew, had been one of those hearts.

"Margaret, it is so good to see you!" Augusta smiled as Emmy slipped quietly out of the room.

"I am so happy to be included in this homecoming. Will it be just your family?"

"Yes, but it's possible Joseph's friend, Michael Lewis, will be traveling with him." Augusta leaned against her bedpost as Margaret sat at the vanity.

"Michael Lewis?" Margaret chuckled unkindly. "I'd be surprised if he were able to leave his precious school. Such an uptight, intellectual, uninteresting sort. At least he won't bore us with any drivel. I bet he still won't be able to talk in our presence."

Augusta giggled, though she didn't want to make fun of the shy cadet. If Joseph was friends with Michael, it must be for a good reason. She changed the subject.

"I am so excited to see Joseph." Augusta patted her hair. "I find it hard to believe that he has been gone for four years already."

"I cannot believe it either." Margaret looked at her perfect reflection in the mirror and smiled. "Perhaps now, he will be willing to settle down with me."

Augusta sat on her bed and looked at her friend with concern in her eyes. "Margaret, it has recently come to my attention that...well, I found out that..."

"Does Joseph have another girl?" Margaret spun around.

"No, I don't think Joseph is ready to settle down. Not yet, at least."

"That's too bad." Margaret looked at her friend. "You see, I just, ohhh...can I confide in you about something, Augusta?"

"Of course."

Margaret stood and walked to the bed, flounced down next to Augusta and turned to face her friend. "Father says that things are not going well with our family finances. Apparently, he made some poor investments. He needs me to marry, and soon."

"Well, then Joseph is not your man, not if that's your goal. As I said, he's not ready to settle down and he may never be terribly wealthy."

"Wealth isn't the most important aspect. Prestige and power can be much more enticing, and he will surely get that as an officer in the US Army."

"That may be true, but if your father needs money..."

"Could you please talk to him, Augusta?" Tears appeared in Margaret's eyes. "I need a husband. If I don't find one soon, father is likely to arrange a marriage for me."

"I honestly don't know about Joseph, he can be so unpredictable. Margaret...how do you feel...I mean...what about Andrew?"

"Andrew? He's nice enough, I suppose. A little boring and stuffy, but he's definitely handsome. Why do you ask?"

Augusta thought about her oldest brother, she tried to picture him as a suitor would. Of average height, Andrew was the picture of a perfect Southern gentleman. He had black hair, the hazel eyes that ran in the Byron family, and a soft, kind smile. He was proper, almost to a fault, and always kind and gentle. Being the oldest brother, he had been raised to take over the family plantation. He was already taking over many responsibilities of running the business from their father. He would be the ideal match for Margaret.

"I recently learned that Andrew has had feelings for you for years. He just never thought you were ready for marriage, much less marriage to him. If I were to perhaps tell him that you are interested, well, I'm sure he would speak to your father, maybe even make an offer for your hand."

"Would he, now?" Margaret smiled. "That just might work."

Though she had suggested it, an uncomfortable feeling coursed through Augusta at Margaret's immediate acquiescence. She knew that marrying well was a young woman's main objective, and both of her brothers were considered fine catches, as was the man courting Augusta herself, but something didn't feel right.

"By the by, you will have the opportunity to finally meet Mr. Jeffrey Cullen tomorrow at the reception." Augusta smoothed her skirts, glowing at the thought of being able to see Jeffrey again. She had met him in Charleston over six months ago, and he had come by Byron Hill at least once a week to court her, but Margaret had been in Georgia visiting family for most of that time and had yet to meet the lawyer who had swept Augusta off her feet.

"Splendid!" Margaret smiled. "I have been looking forward to meeting him for quite some time. You wrote the most delectable things about him in your letters while I was away."

"He is a very special man," Augusta replied. A knock at the door interrupted her next words, and Emmy entered the room again.

"Pardon me, Miz Augusta, but yo brother and Mista Lewis be here. They's waitin' fo the both of ya in the parlor."

"Thank you, Emmy." Augusta smiled and stood. "Well, shall we go and welcome the cadets home?"

Margaret took Augusta's arm. "That sounds like a perfect idea."

Michael Lewis took a sip of the brandy that Joseph had given him. He didn't usually drink alcohol, but didn't want to offend his hosts. It was his first time south of the Mason-Dixon Line, and he had quickly learned that the culture down here was almost that of a foreign nation.

"Pardon me, sirs." A pretty black girl, around his own age, entered the parlor. "Miz Augusta and Miz Margaret will be down directly."

Michael took another sip of the brandy. Perhaps the alcohol could give him some Dutch Courage. He had never been comfortable with the ladies, but he had never been tongue-tied to dumbness as he had been with Augusta Byron when he met her in New York two years ago. He could only hope and pray that the same thing wouldn't happen this time. He had never met anyone so lovely. She seemed to tug at his heart, and was someone he actually wanted to spend the rest of his life with. It was silly, he realized that. He barely knew the girl, and Joseph had insinuated that she had a beau here in South Carolina. Perhaps his chance had already been lost.

"Joseph!" Augusta's excited squeal pulled Michael's focus to the beautiful young woman he was thinking of. He stood and studied her, trying not to be too obvious. She looked radiant, as he had expected. Her blonde hair pulled back, with ringlets curling down. Those striking green eyes. She was taller than most women, but that didn't bother him, as he was taller than most men.

Augusta hugged her brother tightly, then turned and smiled at Michael, slight surprise in her eyes.

"Miss Byron. It is a pleasure to see you again." His heart pounded being in her presence again. He hoped his voice sounded strong and confident. He took two steps towards her and took her hand in his. Mustering all of his courage, he bent down and kissed her hand like a debonair gentleman in a Jane Austen novel, the ones his mother and her friends all raved about back home in Gettysburg.

"Mr. Lewis, it is a pleasure to see you too. I am so glad that you were able to come down and visit us." She smiled as he reluctantly released her hand. "I wish Joseph would have told us he was bringing company."

"Why, Mr. Lewis, I daresay, I almost didn't recognize you." Augusta's friend, Miss Margaret, as he remembered from their visit to West Point, tittered. Miss Margaret Wiggs, a woman who hadn't tried to hide the fact that she wanted Joseph Byron to court her. "And it is also quite amazing to hear the change in your voice." Miss Wiggs gave him a smile that was beautiful, but not genuine, not at all like Augusta's. Michael had been taken with Miss Augusta from the moment he met her, and seeing her again reinforced the knowledge that she still was the woman of his dreams. Perhaps he should give himself a chance to win her affections. It would likely be best to start as her friend, however.

"I'm afraid I was a little speechless the last time we met." Michael wished he had a slew of suave words to say to her, but he didn't. "I had never before met a woman so lovely." He spoke to Margaret, yet his eyes didn't leave Augusta's.

"Well, I am delighted that you were able to come down for a visit. It will be such a joy to have you around for the rest of the week. You will be at Joseph's reception tomorrow, won't you?" Augusta asked.

"I will, and thank you, Miss Augusta, though my mother was a little miffed that I chose to spend my time down here and not home in Gettysburg. She does understand, however."

"She's likely just disappointed that she won't be able to see you." Augusta was an expert at making conversation.

"You're right, of course," he replied.

An older black woman entered the room. "Excuse me, but dinner's ready for ya'all." She nodded.

"I hope Keturah made her cornbread." Joseph smiled. "I have been wanting some since I left for the Point."

"Keturah, she know that. O' course she made cornbread for ya, Mista Joseph." The woman grinned.

"Thank you, Dianna," Augusta smiled, then turned to Michael. "Mr. Lewis, you being our special guest, would you do me the honor of escorting me to the dining table?"

"It would be my pleasure, Miss Byron," he replied, then took her offered arm and led her through the doorway.

Saturday, June 27, 1857
Byron Hill Plantation

"I must say, Mista Michael Lewis is not quite what ya described ta me." Emmy said as she pulled at the strings of Augusta's corset. Augusta gripped the bedpost as the undergarment tightened.

"He has changed quite a bit. To be honest, I almost didn't recognize him," Augusta admitted. She thought back to the first day that she had met her brother's best friend. It had been in New York, at the West Point Military Academy. Augusta, her father, Margaret and Andrew had met Joseph for dinner. Michael came as well. Joseph had made his apologies for not writing more, then introduced his friend from Gettysburg. Augusta had been surprised that her brother had befriended a Yankee, and she was even more surprised that the young man wouldn't even make eye contact.

"He still seems quiet and studious, but I must admit, I find those qualities endearing," Augusta said, thinking of Michael's current appearance. He still had dark brown hair and warm brown eyes, yet his gangly physique had now filled out, and was quite muscular. His oval face was covered with a well-trimmed beard and mustache. It was refreshing to hear him talk, though he likely would never dominate a conversation. Augusta actually enjoyed the discussions she had with him last night over dinner. Her heart warmed when she thought about his expressed desire for her to save a dance for him tonight.

"I know ya have your heart set on Mista Jeffrey, but if that don't work out, I think Mista Michael would be a good man for ya ta marry."

"Never say so!" Augusta exclaimed. "He's a good man to be sure, but strange, Joseph told me much the same thing. He believes Michael would be a good match for me too, but Heavens! That would not work at all."

"And why not?" Her maidservant persisted.

"Well, he's in the military for one. You know as well as I do that I am expected to marry someone of means. He has no important connections, Joseph told me his parents run a general store, for goodness sake. And besides that, he's a Yankee, that practically makes him a foreigner down here." She placed a hand on her corset as Emmy tied the undergarment. "No, Michael Lewis is a gentleman, and I will have no problem being friends with him, but don't get it in your head that it will ever be anything more." She turned and stepped into her crinoline.

"If that's what ya say," Emmy replied, pulling the skirt up and tying it around Augusta's waist.

"It most certainly is." Augusta held her arms out as Emmy slipped an underskirt on her body. As kind as Michael Lewis was, there was no way he could keep her in the comforts she was accustomed to. Would she have to get dressed without a maidservant? She pondered that thought, then shook her head. Why was she even thinking these thoughts? Jeffrey had been dropping some not-so-subtle hints about asking for her hand. Anyways, a man like Michael, so good and kind despite his shyness, likely had a sweetheart waiting for him in Gettysburg.

Augusta adjusted her skirts, then sat at her vanity so Emmy could work a miracle on her hair. "Besides, Emmy, I have my future all planned. Don't you worry about me."

Byron Hill Plantation Grounds

Joseph and Michael had gone for a brisk ride over the plantation grounds. Michael pulled hard on the borrowed horse's reins. He had never been much of a rider in his youth, growing up in a town, but he had improved his ability at West Point. He was now quite efficient handling most any horse. He had Joseph to thank for that. It was one of the skills that Joseph had helped him develop. Michael had the distinct feeling that the Byron brothers had been born on horses.

"Does your sister do much riding?" Michael asked, unable to get the blonde-haired beauty out of his mind. Their mounts began to walk slowly back to the stables as they cooled down from the vigorous ride.

"No, not really," Joseph replied. "Not sure why, she learned, of course, but she never took to horses the way Andrew and I did. She is quite good at it, though. No, Augusta likes to stay indoors for the most part, though she does enjoy working in the gardens." He grinned in a teasing manner. "It's probably all my fault. She likely got tired of my pestering her. When she's out in the sun too much, she develops the cutest freckles. She hates it."

"The teasing?"

"And the freckles." Joseph shot him an interested look. "Is there a particular reason you're asking? Do you want to ask Augusta to go riding with you?"

"What if I did? How would you feel about that?"

"Well, I like you a sight better than the man she's courting now." Joseph shook his head. "He's too pompous and arrogant in my opinion."

"I wouldn't want to step in over someone else's territory," Michael replied.

"No, of course you wouldn't," Joseph said. "You're far too polite."

"It's not that, I just wouldn't want to make things difficult for your sister. That is, if she really likes this suitor."

"Unfortunately, I think she does," Joseph sighed.

"Not to mention, even if I thought I had a chance with her, your father probably wouldn't welcome a suit from a Yankee soldier."

"That's true enough. Maybe a Yankee banker or investor, but not a soldier." Joseph shrugged. "As much as I like you, Michael, I fear my father wouldn't consider you a good match for my sister."

"What if I were a soldier from the South?" Michael wasn't sure why he asked that. Joseph was surprised as well.

"I hardly believe you would change your loyalties from the North to the South. I realize with this persistent talk of secession, you would definitely be pro-union!"

Their horses continued walking along the beautiful, palmetto-lined drive. Byron Hill was quite extensive and impressive. It made the small lot that the Lewis General Store sat on pale in comparison.

You're right there, I wouldn't fight for any other army than the United States," Michael admitted. "Though I believe secession will happen sooner or later and an armed conflict will follow."

"You don't really believe our country would go to war with each other just because Carolina wants to secede, do you? That would be madness." Joseph laughed off the idea.

"There have been a lot of unresolved issues over the past ten years that may lead to more than any of us realize. Didn't you pay attention in class? Could you not feel the underlying tension, the division, when you were up north? I know I feel a distinct difference down here."

"Has anyone been unkind to you?" Joseph asked.

"No, not really." Michael admitted. "Just a feeling I get."

"I know we've never really talked about this, I have always just swept it under the rug, but I suppose I can admit to you now that there was definitely some animosity from a few of the cadets. Lawrence Gilbert comes to mind, I just tried to ignore it."

"Now that doesn't surprise me a bit, you are quite good at ignoring problems," Michael said. Joseph was one of the most carefree men he knew. "However, you must admit, there are issues. The nullification conflict back in the '30's, when South Carolinians talked about seceding because of President Jackson's tariff, then there are all of the

Congressional compromises unwinding, and of course, the Fugitive Slave Act. Now with this book, *Uncle Tom's Cabin*, bringing the slavery issue to light, it may possibly divide our country." Michael didn't know why he felt the need to bring all the nation's problems up now.

"Slavery." Joseph's jaw tightened slightly. "I know you're against it, but..."

"Of course I'm against it. It's morally wrong."

"I can see where you would say that, and I know we've discussed this before, but I'm of the mind that we take care of our slaves. I've never witnessed any abuse of our people. It's no reason for anyone to start a war over. Besides, I believe the practice will die out eventually."

"People have already lost their lives over the issue of slavery in Kansas."

"Yes, only because of that lunatic John Brown. He and his sons massacred those pro-slavery settlers at the Pottawatomie Creek." Joseph was trying to hold his temper.

"In response to the sacking of Lawrence earlier that month," Michael retorted.

"How can you defend that murderer?" Joseph shook his head.

"I'm not trying to argue with you, Joseph, I just..." He shook his head. "This is exactly why I'm afraid a war may be imminent. No one can agree, everyone strongly believes they are right. I tell you, Joseph,

I've made a few good friends from the south, you being one of them. I would hate to have to fight against any of you."

"Again, I don't think it will come to all that," Joseph replied. "Listen, Michael, I know you have your opinions, and there is no one I would rather discuss the issues with. But would you mind terribly not discussing them with my family? My father and brother are much more opinionated about our Southern way of life than I am."

"Of course. I would never want to be the cause of a commotion, not when you've all been such gracious hosts." Michael nodded as the stables came into view. "You're likely the only Southerner I would talk about this subject with."

"Thank you for understanding," Joseph replied. "You may be a Yankee, but for some reason, you make a darn good friend."

Byron Hill Plantation Ballroom

Augusta smiled as she looked around the room. Many friends from Charleston and surrounding plantations had come to wish Joseph well. He had been assigned to the US Cavalry and would be sent west in a fortnight. She would miss him dearly again, though his four years at West Point had given her time to get used to the idea of not having him around.

"I see your intended is dancing with Miss Margaret Wiggs." Michael Lewis stepped next to her. He looked handsome with his dark hair parted to the side and styled with pomade. He wore his Military Academy dress grays very well.

"Yes, I introduced them earlier today and they seem to be getting on quite well, I'm very pleased to say. It is important that my future husband and my very dearest friend like each other. Besides, if Margaret has anything to say about it, she'll be a part of our family before long."

"I see," Michael said with a slight smirk. "Which brother does she have her sights set on?"

"I'll give you one guess."

Michael looked over at Joseph, who was smiling and flirting with another friend of Augusta's, Azalea Harris.

"I would guess Joseph, though I know he has no intention of settling down anytime soon, so I believe Andrew would be a better match for her."

"Which is exactly what I told her. I also am fairly certain that Andrew is quite smitten with her."

"Margaret is pretty enough, I suppose, but not half as beautiful as you." Michael spoke quickly and quietly, almost as if he wasn't confident about saying it aloud.

"Why, Mr. Lewis, you can speak quite charmingly when you want to."

"I suppose." His face reddened. "I wonder, perhaps..." he hesitated and looked down, which should have been annoying, but was actually quite sweet to her. Looking back up, he met her smiling face. "Miss Byron, would you care to dance with me?"

"I would love to," Augusta replied, taking his offered arm. She had hoped he would ask. She brushed the maroon silk taffeta of her ball gown. Her bodice was trimmed with a white ruffled lace collar that draped the edge of her shoulders. She loved the dress and was delighted to have the opportunity to wear it to the ball with so many people in attendance. She placed one gloved hand on his shoulder and he took her other hand in his, gingerly placing his free hand on her waist. The band started a waltz, and they began moving together. His steps were a bit unsure, but his effort was apparent.

"I must apologize, Miss Byron. I'm not the best dancer. In fact, I may be the least accomplished man here."

"Nonsense, you're performing quite admirably." She smiled, trying to put him at ease. "I can't imagine you have much call to practice your dancing at West Point."

"No, indeed not, and I was never much for attending social events in my hometown."

"Too buried in your books, I suppose." She teased.

"Guilty, as charged," he replied. "I have always wanted to attend West Point and knew I must study hard to do so."

"That's not how Joseph tells it. He says you graduated at the top of your class, even smarter than he is and that's saying a lot. He says that other than being a better horseman, you and he were quite the equals."

"We helped each other succeed, to be sure. I daresay there were some courses we both struggled with and if not for us studying and working together, we would not have been so successful. I must say though, that he helped me with the physical aspects of the West Point education. I never had formal training in horsemanship, fencing, or marksmanship. I didn't need such activities living in a small town. I learned quickly though, with Joseph's help."

"Why did you decide to go there?" Augusta asked.

"It is one of the best colleges around. There is a small college in Gettysburg, but I always liked the idea of serving my country like many of my ancestors did. I can now do that with my West Point education.

I have been assigned to the Corps of Engineers, though I sometimes wonder if being in the cavalry with Joseph wouldn't be more exciting."

"I am sure it would be, but I have a feeling you'll be well-received in whatever branch you are assigned, based on what Joseph has told us."

"Thank you for saying so." Michael smiled. Too soon, the dance ended, and feeling bold, Michael brought Augusta's hand up for a gentle kiss. "And thank you for honoring me with a dance."

"Of course." She smiled, then glanced around, looking for Margaret and Mr. Cullen. "Fie, I wonder where Margaret has run off to."

"Are you looking for Margaret?" Joseph asked as he approached Michael and Augusta, Miss Azalea Harris on his arm.

"I saw her walking towards the hallway with a gentleman," Azalea said. "I'm not quite sure who he was, though."

"Oh, thank you, Azalea." Augusta nodded as Joseph introduced Michael to Azalea.

"Augusta, are you alright?" Joseph asked.

"I'm fine, I just need to rest for a moment. Will you please excuse me?" Augusta smiled, then headed off in the direction of her father's study. It was much quieter there so she sat down, gazing out the window. She loved the view from here, looking out over the Cooper River, just as the sun was setting. It was sad to know that one day she would have to leave her home. Perhaps sooner, rather than later, if things progressed with Jeffrey Cullen the way she believed they would. Such a charming man.

The door of the study was suddenly knocked open and a couple stumbled into the room, arms around each other, kissing quite passionately. Augusta sprang to her feet, shocked by the display. It was hard to distinguish the couple as the lighting was poor inside and the couple was so engrossed in each other, they didn't even notice her.

"I beg your pardon!" Augusta cried out as the couple tumbled to a settee. The man pulled himself off the woman and Augusta's heart hammered when she saw who it was.

"Mr. Cullen!" She looked at the woman, who had sat up on the settee. Hurt and betrayal coursed through her. "Margaret!" She didn't know what shocked her more: finding her best friend in the amorous embrace of the man she was courting or finding the man she was courting in her best friend's embrace.

"Miss Byron, of course, I can explain..." Jeffrey stood tall and poised.

"Explain?!" Augusta's voice cracked as tears welled up in her eyes. All of her hopes and dreams collapsed as she looked at her dearest friend... "I'm quite sure I need no explanation. None at all!" She wiped her tears and started to dash out of the room, needing to get away.

"He asked for my hand in marriage, Augusta." Margaret's words stopped Augusta at the doorway. She turned, tears falling down her cheeks. Margaret stood next to Jeffrey, taking his arm. "We're going to be married."

Augusta looked at Jeffrey, the man she had been ready to pledge her life to. He stood there, clearly embarrassed, but he said nothing in opposition to Margaret's words. Not knowing what to say, Augusta fled the study, the need to get away even more essential.

Out of the corner of his eye, Michael saw a flash of maroon, the color of the dress Augusta was wearing. He smiled politely and excused himself from talking with Joseph and a few other gentlemen. He was fairly certain Augusta was rushing out of the house and she looked quite upset. When he exited the house, he looked around, but didn't see her.

"Miss Byron, where did you go?" He whispered to himself, then quickly remembered that Joseph had mentioned Augusta loved spending time in the gardens. He followed a lantern-lit pathway that turned toward the general direction of the gardens.

"Miss Byron?" He quietly called out, then listened for a response. He heard some muffled sniffling and hastened towards the sounds. "Miss Byron?" He turned a corner and saw her sitting on a wrought-iron bench. She tried to hide her tears from him, but it was no use.

"Mr. Lewis, pray tell, what are you doing out here?" She scrunched a handkerchief in her hand.

"I saw you rush out of the house, you looked quite distressed. Whatever happened to upset you so? You were fine just a few minutes ago when we were dancing. I do hope it wasn't anything I said or did."

Augusta's head snapped up. "You mustn't think that, Michael! You have done nothing wrong." The use of his first name told him just how upset she was. He liked hearing it in her genteel Southern accent, though.

Augusta looked toward the house. "I don't believe you would ever do anything that would upset me in this way." Tears fell from her eyes and as she raised her handkerchief to wipe her tears, her shaking hands caused her to drop the cloth. "Oh, botheration." She reached down to pick it up, but Michael reached it first and gently put it in her palm. She sighed when she saw how dirty it had gotten. "Fiddlesticks." She wiped her cheeks with her gloved hand.

"Miss Byron, please allow me." He pulled out his own handkerchief and handed it to her.

"Thank you, you are most kind." She took it and wiped her eyes.

"Of course," he said. "Now, are you ready to talk about what's troubling you?"

"I don't know that I'll ever want to discuss it, it is much too devastating, but I suppose. You and everyone else will find out eventually anyways." She took a shaky breath to calm her nerves. "I have just lost my hopes and dreams, the future I had planned, at least in my heart, the man who has just..."

"What did he do to you?" Uncharacteristic anger coursed through him at the thought of someone hurting Augusta in any way, and if Jeffrey Cullen had somehow... Michael stood, ready to go find the bastard and...

Augusta grabbed his arm. "Michael, no. It's not what you're thinking, or what I believe you're thinking, at least. He just... He has betrayed me, and to be honest, his betrayal doesn't sting nearly as much as who he was betraying me with. Ohh, that doesn't make any sense, even to me."

Michael did, however, comprehend what she was saying. "May I ask who that person is?"

She shook her head, tears welling up again. "My dear friend, Margaret, if you can believe that."

Fresh anger consumed Michael. How could Mr. Cullen and Miss Wiggs treat Augusta in this manner? How could Mr. Cullen just throw Augusta's affections away? How could Margaret do this to her best friend? They had just been introduced, hadn't they? What were they thinking? "I am so sorry, Miss Byron. You don't deserve to be treated in this manner, not at all."

"Thank you for saying so." Augusta sniffed and took a deep breath. "I feel so foolish. I should have noticed the signs, I must have missed something or refused to see it. I was under the impression they had never met before today, but she told me...Margaret told me that Jeffrey made her an offer of marriage, and he didn't deny it." Tears continued to fall from her eyes. "I am so stupid, I should have expected something. Jeffrey needs connections and Margaret's father has an abundance of those, and on the other side of the coin, Margaret's family needs her to marry into money and Jeffrey has that. Oh, I should have realized it, the way they were talking and...argh... It is an ideal match."

"In your world, perhaps. Not everywhere."

"I just thought Jeffery and I would be together forever. I thought we had a future." She shook her head. "I never dreamed he would betray me, much less with my best friend. She met Michael's eyes. I would never betray you, Augusta. He wanted to tell her.

"Well, I must say that Mr. Cullen doesn't deserve you. Neither does Miss Wiggs, as a friend. As hard as this might be for you to hear, it's a good thing this happened now and not later. It's good you discovered Cullen's true character before it was too late."

"I know you're right here," Augusta sighed and pointed to her head, then moved her hand to her heart. "but here it is not comprehending why two people I thought cared about me, would hurt me so much just for power and money." Augusta swept at the tears on her cheeks again, then wiped her nose. "You're right though, I would never want to be tied to a man who would stray. And Margaret...perhaps I should have been more aware of what she was capable of. I certainly knew she needed an advantageous marriage, but I heard..." She sat up as if suddenly realizing something. "Oh, dear. Andrew's heart will be broken as well." She shook her head and took a deep breath. "But, as you said, at least we found all this out now."

"And you will become a better person for going through this," Michael reminded her. "You'll be smarter and stronger."

"That is so kind of you to say. You are the best confidant I could have asked for." She placed a gloved hand on his forearm. "Thank you for coming out here, Mr. Lewis. You don't know how much I appreciate what you've done for me tonight."

"What are friends for?" He smiled, then bowed his head. "My apologies, Miss Byron. I shouldn't have been so presumptuous."

"You don't presume too much at all. I would be proud to call you a friend." She smiled. "And if that's the case, then we should abandon some formalities, especially since you are my brother's best friend. You must call me Augusta."

"Of course. And I would be pleased to have you call me Michael."

"It seems strange to say this, with everything that I have been through tonight, but I am glad we were able to have this conversation. I suppose something good can come of something bad."

"Indeed. That is how God works. I do want you to know that I will be keeping you in my prayers as you work your way through this difficulty."

"I...all right. Thank you."

Michael smiled. He discovered long ago that the Byron family wasn't very devout. He had been encouraging Joseph to attend church for the past three years with some minor success. It appeared he should work on Augusta as well.

"But of course." He smiled, then stood. "How are you feeling? Do you think you are ready to go back in? With you always being the belle of the ball, I'm sure you have been missed."

"Goodness. Unfortunately, you're probably right." She stood and took his offered arm. "I suppose I will have to face Margaret and Mr. Cullen eventually. Let's get this over with." She gripped his arm tightly and he knew she was nervous to return to the party. "Dear me, I must look frightful."

"Have no fear, Augusta. I will not leave your side until you want me to." He averted his eyes, "and you still look beautiful."

She flashed him a grateful smile. "You already seem to know me better than Mr. Cullen did," she said quietly as they walked up the steps to the house. He squeezed her hand, which rested on his arm.

"Again, Jeffrey Cullen is a fool for letting you get away from him."

"You're too kind," Augusta replied. "Much kinder than I deserve."

"Augusta, there you are." The pretty blonde, Miss Azalea Harris, approached them. "Are you all right? The whole party is abuzz with news of the engagement of Miss Wiggs and Mr. Cullen. No one can believe it, seeing as though we all believed he would be making an offer of marriage to you."

"Yes, it was quite a shock," Augusta admitted. "But I'm sure I will survive the disappointment, with the help of my true friends." She smiled at Michael, whose heart warmed. "Where is the happy couple?"

"They both departed already, she with her family and he on his own."

"Well, I suppose that's a relief. Something I don't have to deal with quite yet."

"I imagine that when you do run into them, you will handle the encounter with grace and poise, as always." Michael patted her gloved hand.

"I must say, you have a much better opinion of me than I do of myself." Augusta smiled at Michael again. He smiled back and thanked God for the opportunity to become the friend of this young woman.

Monday, July 6, 1857
Byron Hill Plantation

The next week found Augusta reflecting on the events that had happened the night of Joseph's reception. She had received a note from Jeffrey Cullen, apologizing for any confusion or misconceptions about their relationship. It was, as Michael remarked when she shared it with him, a stuffy and impersonal correspondence. She had also received a visit from Margaret, who acted as though nothing untoward had happened. Augusta didn't want to discuss the issue, and tried to believe that all had happened for a reason, as Michael had told her. She had quickly realized that she was better off without Jeffrey, but it was worse with Margaret. Discovering exactly what kind of person she really was after all the years as friends still made Augusta's heart ache. While she tried her best to be cordial during the visit, it was a cold and stuffy affair and was cut short after an offer of tea.

Her family had been helpful, but Michael Lewis had been her rock throughout the ordeal. He was so kind and comforting, such a gentleman. What surprised her the most was that she was actually handling the situation better than she thought with the help of her family and she found that Michael was becoming a very good friend.

"I cannot believe you're leaving already." Augusta said as she walked Michael to the door. "It's been so nice getting to know you, especially this past week."

"I quite agree," Michael said. "I must say, you are so easy to talk with. I have enjoyed all of our conversations."

"That was not the case the first time I met you in New York." She smiled kindly.

"Yes, well, I'm glad I no longer have that problem."

"I'm glad as well." Augusta was just about to open the door and walk down the steps with Michael to the circle drive. Gideon was to bring Joseph's stallion and a horse for Michael, so that Joseph could bring Michael to the nearby train stop and see him off.

"Miz Augusta, Mista Lewis." Stephen, Andrew's manservant, approached the two.

"What is it, Stephen?" Augusta asked.

"I was sent ta tell ya that Mista Joseph is feeling poorly and can't bring Mista Lewis ta the train stop."

"Goodness, what about Father or Andrew?" Augusta asked.

"They both rode inta Charleston early this morning fo' business. Mista Joseph is requestin' that ya'll bring Mista Lewis ta the station an see him off so's he has a family member ta accompany him stead a just Gideon."

"What? Unchaperoned?" Augusta placed a hand on her upper chest. "And besides, I won't have time to change into my riding habit."

"Yes, ma'am, I just sent Jordan back ta the stables ta have Gideon hitch up the buggy. Joseph say Gideon can drive ya so's ya'll be escorted."

"Well, Joseph did think of everything." Augusta put a nervous hand to her stomach, unsure of why she was skittish to be alone with Michael. "All right, then, that's fine. I'll have Emmy fetch my hat and we'll be off." She turned to Michael. "I hope this is suitable to you."

"Of course." He nodded as she turned and hastened up the stairs. "But I would still like to go up and tell Joseph goodbye, thank him again for his hospitality."

"Yes sir, Mista Lewis, he felt ya would say that, but he be quite indisposed an not feeling up ta seeing anyone. He send his apologies, an wishes ya safe travels. He be stopping in Washington City when he reports in with his regiment befo' heading west an say he be sure ta look ya up."

"That's comforting, at least. Thank you Stephen." Michael nodded as Augusta returned to his side. They walked out the door, toward the circle drive where a hefty black man in his forties stood by a buggy. Michael's bags had already been loaded by the slave.

"You do know you needn't worry about me, and you don't need to accompany me." Michael placed his hat on his head. "I've no need of an escort, especially with a driver to take me."

"Nonsense," Augusta took his arm. "I have nothing pressing today. I would enjoy a buggy ride and seeing you off, of course."

"All right, then." He helped her into the buggy, then circled it and climbed in the other side. "Thank you, Gideon." The slave snapped the reins and the horses were off.

"Are you looking forward to your post assignment? Washington City, I believe." She asked.

"Yes, Washington, and yes, I am, to be honest," Michael admitted. "But this has been a splendid visit, and I enjoyed getting to know you and your family better."

"I am so glad," Augusta replied. Michael's heart pounded. He had wanted a moment or two with Augusta and now that the opportunity had presented itself, he was nervous about what he wanted to say.

"I especially enjoyed getting to know you better." He finally braved the words.

"And I, you," she said. "I don't know what I would have done if you hadn't been there for me the night of the reception, and you distracting me with all your attention this past week."

"It was certainly my pleasure." He wanted to take her hand in his, but knew it wouldn't be proper. "And

I must admit, I would like to get to know you better. I hesitated to ask when you were being courted by Cullen, but now with that in the past, I was hoping...well, wondering if you would welcome letters from me."

The train stop wasn't far from Byron Hill, and Michael could already see it coming into view. Augusta was quiet for a moment, and he wondered if he had spoken out of turn.

"If I am being to forward and this offer is too soon after..."

She silenced him with a hand on his arm. "No, Michael, it's not. It's quite apparent now that I thought more of our courtship than Jeffery ever did."

"You can't say that. If a man asks a woman to court him, he should realize that means he is serious about marriage and he should not play games with her affections." Michael insisted.

"That is not always the case, surely you know that." The buggy stopped and Gideon hopped out to get Michael's bags. Michael stepped down and went around to help Augusta down. Before he let go of her waist, he gave her a meaningful look.

"It would always be the case with me, Augusta."

Augusta wasn't quite sure how to reply, which was strange for her. She was starting to realize that she may have feelings of a romantic nature for this man and it scared her. He was not the type she would ever consider a serious suitor for so many reasons. The biggest reason being the fact that he was a Yankee and she knew that could be a problem in the future.

"You are an honorable man, Michael Lewis. I know you would never take advantage of anyone or anything." She smiled as he took her arm and lead her up to the platform. She took a deep breath. She supposed it wouldn't hurt to write him, as if he were any other friend who lived far away. "As for your request, I see no reason why we shouldn't write each other. You are a dear friend."

"Splendid," he replied. "Letters may not come with regularity from me, as I will be very busy with my duties, but I will write whenever I can." He led her to a bench and they sat.

"I cannot promise anything terribly exciting as my day to day activities can be quite monotonous, but I will write to you as well." She smiled and faced him. "I must say, I will miss you."

"And I you." Michael took her hand in his and his brown eyes looked into hers. Her heart raced as their eyes locked. She had never felt this way with Jeffery. He had snuck a kiss or two, but this attraction to Michael was so strong and different.

Choo Choo! The whistle and clacking of the train on the tracks interrupted her thoughts.

"Well, then." He stood, not quite ready to be on his way. "I suppose this is goodbye for now." She stood next to him, realizing not for the first time how tall he was. Jeffrey had always made comments about her 'unladylike height', as he was just as tall as she was.

"Travel safe," she said. He bent down to kiss her on the cheek. In an uncharacteristic, impulsive move, Augusta cupped his cheek and moved slightly, so that he met her lips instead. When he pulled away, her face heated, but she wasn't sorry. "I look forward to hearing from you, Mr. Lewis." The train chugged to a stop.

"All right then." His cheeks had reddened as well. He put his hat back on his head, grabbed his carpet bags and boarded the train. "Goodbye, Miss Byron!"

She stood on the platform as the train pulled out and waited until she could no longer see it.

"Ya 'bout ready, Miz Augusta?" Gideon asked. She blushed even more when she realized that the driver must have witnessed her forwardness. She had no doubt he would tell his wife, Dianna, which wouldn't be so bad, as she fully intended to talk through her feelings with Emmy, who was Dianna's daughter that evening anyway, especially since she had so many conflicting feelings.

Wednesday, August 5, 1857
Byron Hill Plantation

Miss Byron,   *Washington City*

I do wish I could have written sooner, but I had to settle in and start my duties. As it is my first assignment, I am picking up more and more responsibilities, including training new recruits. I enjoyed tutoring your brother and other classmates, and I find that I really enjoy teaching and training others. Perhaps after my time is served in the army, I can find a job at a university as a professor.

I must confess, things aren't all excellent in Washington City. I don't know if you recall a Lawrence Gilbert from your visit to New York, or if your brother ever mentioned him. Unfortunately, he is also stationed here, and he has never liked me very much. He is constantly trying to bully me, it seems. Just the other day, he blamed me for some mistakes that were made in the laboratory. It was his error, of course, and I should have said something to our commanding officer, but I didn't want to play Gilbert's games. I know if I just keep my head down and do my best and work hard, my skills will show my superiors what they need to see, when they need to see it. Your brother always encouraged me to defend myself against Lawrence, but I don't see the point. Men like him won't change or learn. I know that God will take care of me.

I miss you. Sometimes I wonder if your brother was feeling indisposed on purpose the day I left Byron Hill. When he visited me here, he made some comments that led me to believe he wanted you to bring me to the train stop the whole time. I have a hard time seeing Joseph as a matchmaker, but I must admit, the way I'd like our relationship to progress, it is nice to know that one of your family members approves of our friendship. Although again, perhaps I am being too presumptuous. The way that we parted continues to give me hope that I have a future with you. I was pleasantly surprised by your response before I boarded the train. I'd never want to make assumptions, but I do intend on pursuing a relationship with you the right and proper way, as I feel God wants you in my future. Please let me know if you would be agreeable to this.

I must go for now, but I hope to hear from you soon. If I have spoken out of turn, I beg your forgiveness.

Until next time, I remain yours truly,
Michael Lewis

"Is that a letter from Mista Joseph's friend?" Emmy entered the parlor, dustrag in hand.

"Yes, as a matter of fact, it is," Augusta tucked the letter back in the envelope.

"And what does he have ta say?" She asked, working her way around the room, dusting.

"He's just telling me of his duties and sadly, of a fellow officer, a man whom I remember from my visit to West Point and from conversations with Joseph. A man by the name of Lawrence Gilbert."

"A memorable man, then?"

"Yes, but not in a good way," Augusta replied. "He was introduced to me and was quite persistent while we were there, very much a nuisance. He was handsome and charming, but there was something about him that I didn't quite trust." She sighed. "If only I'd had a feeling like that when Jeffrey Cullen first came calling."

"Ya need ta forget about that man, an focus on the one writin' ta ya. If ya askin me, Mista Lewis be a much better man, an he been quite smitten with ya since he set foot in this house." Emmy continued her work.

"Do you really think so?" Augusta asked.

"I's certain bout it as I's been bout anythin'," Emmy replied.

"Perhaps he was even earlier." Augusta thought out loud. "Perhaps Mr. Lawrence Gilbert knew that back then, and that's why he paid so much attention to me. It seems as though this man wants whatever Michael has."

"That's not good," Emmy said, then looked up and smiled when Stephen entered the room.

"Miz Augusta, Emmy." The man smiled, showing white, slightly crooked teeth. "Miz Augusta, Mista

Andrew wants me ta tell ya that he an Mista Ian are goin' inta Charleston for business. They won't be back 'til afta supper."

"All right, thank you, Stephen," Augusta said. Stephen nodded and smiled at Emmy, then left.

"I suppose I now have some uninterrupted time. I believe I'll head to the library and respond to Mr. Lewis's letter, and perhaps even write to Joseph as well." She thought of Joseph's parting words, *Take care of yourself, Augusta, and make sure you don't dwell on Jeffrey Cullen too much longer.* "My brother has some explaining to do as well."

Thursday, September 17, 1857
Byron Hill Plantation
My dearest Augusta,

I received your last letter. I must say, I was quite proud that you have forgiven Miss Wiggs and Mr. Cullen. That reinforces my belief of just how beautiful a woman you are. I also appreciate each and every letter you send. It is the highlight of my week. You may think you have nothing important to write about, but I find that you have an amazing way of telling stories, almost lyrical.

There have been some interesting developments in our country. I know you don't follow the news closely, but with my current assignment, I feel as though I must inform you. Especially with good friends like your brother Joseph serving in Texas.

In case you didn't know there is a war going on out west. Last year, President Buchanan sent U.S. forces to the Utah Territory for expansion purposes. The Mormons, a religious cult living out there, became fearful that the military force had been sent to annihilate them. Since they have faced persecution in other areas of the country, they prepared to defend themselves.

The Mormons blocked the army's entrance into the Salt Lake Valley, and weakened the U.S. Army by preventing them from receiving provisions.

A few days ago, settlers from Arkansas, Missouri and other states were heading to California. They were all killed by a group of local Mormon militiamen. The Mormons first claimed that the migrants were killed by Indians, but that was not the case. If I am not mistaken, Joseph could possibly be transferred from his current post to Utah. Not all of our country's problems are here in the east.

Also, I must ask if you have heard of the sinking of the SS Central America off the coast of North Carolina. How horrible, to lose 425 lives during a hurricane. I must admit, I never thought to fear for you and your family on the coast until hearing this story. I do hope you've never been in danger due to one of these horrific storms.

In more personal news, overall, my life is going well here in Washington, though I am looking forward to my transfer, which most likely will be Harper's Ferry, Virginia. As much as I enjoy Washington City, I am looking forward to the change in scenery.

There is another reason I am anxious to transfer. When I do so, I feel I will be able to start really thinking about my future. I hope my words won't be unwelcome, but I would like to write to your father and ask him permission to formally court you. That is, if you are agreeable. If you prefer not, I will be devastated, but will still remain your friend. I would rather have your friendship than nothing, but Augusta, I want you to know that I care for you a great deal and I thank God every day that He put you in my life.

I know that it is still a long ways away, and much could happen between now and then, but I would be honored if you could come visit me. It would be splendid to see you and your father again. Please let me know if that is something you would possibly want to do.

You asked in your last letter about my relationship with my parents. I love them both dearly, and Mother is extremely supportive, but I must confess, I've always believed my father could have done more with his life, other than just running a general store in Gettysburg. His own father was a military man and Father could have gone to the Point and gotten the best of educations. I have never been able to broach the subject with him of why he made this decision though. I'm fairly certain you're the only person I've ever told this to. What it is about you that I find myself sharing so many thoughts with you that I have never shared with anyone else, whether in person or in writing.

I realize now that this letter is full of questions and thoughts, I hope it hasn't been too much for you to consider.

I remain your friend,
Michael Lewis

"Miz Augusta, what seems ta be troubling ya?" Dianna asked when Augusta put the letter down. "I thought ya'll be happy ta get a letter from that young man."

"I am. It's always pleasant to hear from Michael." That much was true. Augusta loved receiving his letters. She kept them all in a special box in her room and would often re-read them. He always knew what she needed to hear, and it was very comforting to know that she could write him about anything and everything. With most friends and acquaintances, she never felt she could write all of her true thoughts and feelings, but with Michael, she felt confident doing so. At least almost everything.

"So den what be the problem?" As always, Dianna was too perceptive.

"I like him, very much, perhaps too much." She held up the letter. "He wants to ask Father permission to court me, and he has made it perfectly clear that when he asks a girls to court him, it's one step away from asking permission to marry him."

"Well, if'n ya like him, and he want ta court ya, ya shouldna have a problem. I still stuck on how ya'll said ya might be likin' him too much. Not sure that be possible." Dianna put her hands on her hips. "Why would ya not want ta marry that boy? He smart, he kind, he be right handsome."

"He is all that, and more," Augusta admitted. "But Dianna, I have always been told, been taught that is, that I need a marriage that will benefit me and my family."

"That be the truth. But it appear ta me that ya'll and Mista Michael have somethin' special. Emmy told me ya consider him a very good friend."

"I do," Augusta said quietly.

"If ya ask me, that be the most important thing."

Augusta bit her lip, a nervous habit. She appreciated Dianna's advice, as always. "Yes, but Dianna, as I said, you know as well as I do that I am expected to marry a wealthy Southern gentleman with prospects, a man from a good family."

"Ahh, yes. A man like Jeffrey Cullen? That boy, he be far from perfect for ya'll." Dianna shook her head. "Miz Augusta, I gotta say, there's some things that are more important than wealth and prospects. It not like Mista Michael be white trash, he be a mighty fine gentleman and he already treat ya right and proper."

"I know that." Augusta didn't know how to explain her reservations about marrying Michael, as she didn't understand them completely herself. "There's also the fact that he's a northerner and I'm from South Carolina. With the way things are going in this country, that could get very complicated. We are so different when it comes to certain viewpoints. Not to mention the fact that he is very devoted to his religion and I can't remember the last time I set foot in a church."

"Well, I admit, those reasons do make a bit more sense. It good to know ya be thinking about things. Many girls yo' age fall in and outta love without nary a thought and still marry for money."

"I've done that already and learned my lesson."

"I needs ta say, Miz Augusta, I be very proud of ya for the way ya dealt with that very bad business with Miz Margaret and Mista Cullen. Ya were poised and dignified through the whole affair. Yo mama woulda been proud too."

Augusta felt a pang of sadness at the thought of the mother she never knew. "Thank you for saying that. I...I often think about my conflicts and problems and wonder what she would advise me to do. I hope I do make her proud. Always."

"Ya do, Miz Augusta. I knows ya do."

Thursday, October 29, 1857
Byron Hill Plantation

Augusta loved the autumn season. The weather was just perfect to take a stroll through the gardens or down by the Cooper River without the sun being overbearing. As she was walking back from the river, towards the house, she smiled when she noticed her brother, Andrew, ride in. He dismounted when he saw Augusta walking and joined her.

"How was your ride into Charleston?" Augusta asked.

"If your next question is going to be "did we receive any mail from Mr. Lewis", the answer is no. My apologies."

"It's not your fault, of course, but he hasn't written me in weeks."

"It just feels that way." Andrew chuckled. "I know he wrote to you several days ago."

"Yes, I know." Augusta wouldn't admit it to her brother, but she lived for the days she received word from Michael. She had responded to his previous letter quite positively, telling him that she would welcome his suit and would enjoy coming to visit him. Michael had then immediately written to her father asking permission to court her.

"He also wrote to Father," Andrew stated.

"Yes, I know. I told him that I wanted him to."

"You do realize that a courtship with Michael Lewis is just as good as a proposal. The man is very serious about his relationships."

"I'm aware of that, Andrew. You sound as if you don't approve?"

Andrew removed his hat. "You won't be happy with me, but no, I do not. There are many reasons why I would prefer he not be your husband."

"I suppose his lack of money is your chief concern?" Augusta asked.

"No, actually it is not. The current economic panic we're in has reminded many people, myself included, that money can easily be lost." Recently, the United States and many countries in Europe had fallen into an economic recession. Many families in the area had lost much of their wealth. Andrew continued. "Your former beau is a prime example. The Cullen family took quite a loss."

"I had heard that," Augusta said. "I also heard that they will prevail."

"Yes, despite all of his faults, Jeffrey knows how to deal with money. He'll help his father recover."

"That is good for them." Augusta had been puzzled by her lack of anger at Jeffrey, but when she wrote about it to Michael, he had written back and told her that meant she likely hadn't cared for her former beau as much as she thought. "But I must ask, what are your objections to Michael, then?"

"My biggest concern, and the one that should concern everyone, is that he's a Yankee. Not just a Yankee, but a soldier."

"What does being a soldier have to do with it? Joseph is a soldier."

Jordan, the stable boy, approached the two and Andrew handed him the reins to his stallion. "Joseph has made it clear to me that if it comes down to a war between the states, he will side with his family. Lewis would side with the Union, I am fairly certain you realize this. Would you really want to put yourself in that position? To worry daily about choosing between your families home and your husband?" He shook his head. "I don't want that for my sister, that's for sure."

Augusta bit her lip nervously. "Do you really think it will come to a war? What you're saying, Andrew...do you believe we're heading for...for war?"

"We may be," Andrew said. "I wouldn't be surprised at all. Not soon, but maybe in the next five years or so."

Augusta's heart sank. If what Andrew said was true, a relationship with Michael would prove to be quite difficult. Not only that, if she didn't marry Michael, Augusta had come to the realization that her world would be turned upside down.

"I see you're not as certain now in regards to Michael Lewis," Andrew replied as they walked up the steps to the home.

"No, that's the problem, I am certain of how I feel about Michael, but my major doubts were different than yours. You have given me much to think about."

"It's not that I don't like Michael Lewis. I do. He's been a very good friend to Joseph, and you. I'm glad he was able to distract you from that Jeffrey Cullen fiasco. Under other circumstances, I would encourage Father to welcome the suit, but I just don't want to see you get hurt." Andrew smiled. "You're the best sister a man could ask for."

"Thank you for saying so," Augusta hugged her brother, suddenly feeling very concerned about what the future held.

Part 2: 1858

Tuesday, June 16, 1858
Byron Hill Plantation

Augusta looked out from her position on the front porch at the tree-lined drive. She held a letter from Michael to her lips. She wished she could kiss the man himself, and in a few days, she would be able to do so. Though both her father and her brother had many reservations, Ian Byron was allowing Andrew to escort her to Harper's Ferry. She absolutely could not wait to see Michael. Though she still had her doubts about the progression of the relationship, she knew that seeing Michael would help her make the decisions in regards to her future. With each letter she received from Michael, she fell more in love with him. She smiled to herself and went into the house.

As she walked past her father's open study doorway, he called out to her. "Augusta, dear, will you come in here for a moment?"

She entered the room and hid the letter in between the folds of her dark blue day dress. "Yes, Father?"

"Please, have a seat." He gestured to a chair and she followed his request. He folded his hands on top of the newspaper he had been reading. As she sat, Augusta glanced down at the front page article: Speech of A. Lincoln: Republican Principles.

"I wanted to talk with you about your trip to Harpers Ferry." He cleared his throat. "I have changed my mind. I don't want you to go."

"What? Father, why not? You already agreed..."

"I know what I said. But I am starting to regret even giving Michael permission to court you. If he were to ask for your hand tomorrow, I would not allow it."

"Father, how can you say that? What has happened to cause this change?" She wanted to point out that she was nineteen years old and could make her own decisions, but she wanted to show respect to her father. "I know you had reservations in regards to my relationship with Michael, but you always approved of him as a person."

"I have been thinking on it more and more. I am responsible for your future happiness and I am now convinced that Michael Lewis is not the right husband for you."

Augusta's tried to withhold tears. "Father, please. I'd like you to reconsider. I...I've become very fond of Michael Lewis." Though she wanted to tell her father she was in love with the soldier, she felt she should tell Michael the news first. "Father, what is it exactly you don't approve of?" She had to ask, though she felt she already knew the answer.

"He cannot afford to keep you in the comfort you're accustomed to. If you were to marry Lewis, your life would be drastically altered. No Emmy or any servant to help you in your daily toilet. You may even have to work at that shop his parents own or he would drag you all around the country depending on his military assignments. No more social visits with your friends or leisurely walks through the gardens." He leaned forward. "Not to mention you would likely find yourself in hostile territory since our country cannot reach any compromises. Are you ready for that? Are you 'fond' enough of him to go through all that turmoil? Because if you aren't, well, my dear, once you are married, there will be no going back. I ask you again, Augusta, are you sure?"

With each question Ian asked, Augusta lost confidence. "I...I don't know, Father."

"Good. So you understand why I want you and Andrew to stay here. I also would like you to stop writing to Michael, Augusta. I don't see any good in continuing this relationship."

"Father, please..."

"Read this for yourself!" Ian tossed the paper in front of her. "There's a new political party gaining popularity and one of their leaders is an Illinois lawyer who just gave a fairly interesting speech. Now, I might despise everything this new man and his party stands for, but I agree with one of his main statements. 'A house divided against itself cannot stand.' And that is exactly what your marriage to Michael would be. A house divided. And it will not stand. My dear," he stood and came around the desk and crouched in front of her. "Augusta, I couldn't bear to have that happen to you."

A tear fell down her cheek. Then, her father said the words that truly tugged at her heart.

"And I know your mother wouldn't want you to live a life full of strife either."

"Father, I can't let Michael down. I promised him I would be there. Please let me go. If you want me to be sure, I need to see him. If I need to break off the courtship, I must do it in person." She hoped she didn't sound as though she were begging.

Ian's jaw tightened. Augusta knew her response disappointed her father, but she also knew that her father would eventually give in.

"I'm not going there to marry him, just to visit him, as I would any other friend." She added

Ian stood and rubbed his jaw. "Augusta..."

"Please, Father?"

Ian sighed. "All right. I still have my doubts and I am telling you up front I will never give permission for you two to marry. But I will allow Andrew to escort you to Harpers Ferry, with the intent that you will break off the courtship.

"Thank you, Father." She stood and threw her arms around him. "You don't know how much I appreciate this." She kissed him on the cheek. "I love you."

"And I love you too, my darling girl."

Sunday, June 21, 1858
Harper's Ferry

"Oh, Andrew, I must thank you again. You don't know how grateful I am that you brought me here." Augusta smiled at her brother as they watched the military drills.

"You know I'd do just about anything for you, Augusta," he replied. "I must admit, though, seeing all of this does remind me of how glad I am that I never entered West Point like Joseph."

"No soldier's life for you?" She teased him as she twirled her parasol. They had arrived later than they wanted to, and Augusta hadn't been able to speak with Michael yet.

"No. Not unless something drastic happens," Andrew replied. He then nudged Augusta and pointed to the marching soldiers. "I believe Michael is over there."

She looked to where he pointed and smiled. He was on the opposite side, giving commands. Augusta was anxious to speak with Michael. She knew she had many decisions to make, and talking with Michael would help her see things a bit more clearly.

Before long, the drill was over and the men were dismissed. Augusta wanted to run into Michael's arms, but held back. When she finally neared him, he pulled her into an embrace and kissed her on the cheek.

"I am so glad you're here, Augusta. I was worried something would happen that would prevent you from coming."

"My father did almost change his mind, but I persuaded him." She smiled. "The men in my life always find it difficult to tell me no."

"I'll have to remember that." Michael smiled back.

"You'd better." She leaned closer. "I'd really like it if you were to give me a proper kiss."

He quickly glanced at Andrew, who was speaking with an older gentleman. Michael nodded in their direction. "That may have to wait, my dear. That's my father."

"Goodness." Augusta blushed slightly as Andrew and Mr. Lewis approached them. "Was your mother unable to make it?"

"She came down with an illness the day before they were to leave. My father offered to stay behind, but she insisted he come. Mother wanted a family member to meet the woman I plan to marry. I should be able to visit her as soon as I get my next leave."

"Michael, it's good to see you again." Andrew held his hand out and Michael shook it.

"I'm glad you were able to make it," Michael replied. "Andrew, I see you've already met my father."

"Yes, just now." Andrew nodded.

"Father, I'd like you to meet Miss Augusta Byron. Augusta, this is my father, Mr. Samuel Lewis."

"It's such a pleasure to meet you, Mr. Lewis." Augusta smiled. Samuel Lewis nodded in return. He was shorter than Michael, and Augusta noticed he walked with a limp and carried a cane. His dark hair showed from underneath a black bowler hat and he wore a nice-fitting black suit. He looked every bit a successful businessman.

"The pleasure is all mine," Mr. Lewis replied.

"I look forward to getting to know you over the next few days," Augusta said.

"I would enjoy that as well, unfortunately, I must leave first thing in the morning. My wife, Aideen, is under the weather and I'd like to get back to her as soon as possible."

"Of course. I'm quite sorry. I was looking forward to meeting her."

"She was disappointed as well. She is quite excited to be acquainted with you."

Michael squeezed her hand and smiled. "Well, I reserved a table for us at a local restaurant, so we can at least dine together tonight before you leave in the morning, Father."

"I would be delighted," Mr. Lewis said, and they headed for dinner.

The Banks of the Shenandoah River

That evening, Michael asked Andrew for permission to take Augusta on a walk along the banks of the Shenandoah River.

"I am so proud of you, Michael. Being promoted to Second Lieutenant already! Why didn't you tell me you had earned such an honor? I cannot believe I had to hear it from Joseph."

"I suppose I just didn't want to brag."

She leaned over and kissed his cheek. "Talking of your accomplishments isn't bragging, Michael."

He pulled her closer to him. "Maybe not. I must say, though, I am rather glad Andrew allowed me to take you for a walk. I get the impression he doesn't really want to be here and doesn't approve of our relationship all of a sudden."

"He didn't want to come out here initially. As I mentioned before, I'm quite good at persuading the men in my life to see things my way." She didn't tell Michael that her father wanted her to break off the courtship.

"So you said. I confess, I find it hard to say no to you."

"Mmhmm, I still believe you owe me a kiss from earlier." She pulled at his arm as if she were trying to pull him to a stop.

"I'm aware of that." He smiled. "Just be patient."

"I must say, I find it hard to say no to you as well," she admitted. Michael wanted to puff out his chest with pride and was touched by her words. He realized the power she had just given him with that statement. It humbled him and made him love her all the more. They continued walking in quiet, just content with being together. When they reached a bend in the river, Michael pulled her to a stop.

"This is a beautiful view," she commented. Harpers Ferry was a lovely town. It was situated on a hill in the Blue Ridge Mountains where the Shenandoah River joined the Potomac River. Augusta didn't realize how beautiful the mountains really were.

"Indeed." He smiled. "You know, I never had the chance to stroll with you on Flirtation Walk to the Kissing Rock while I was at West Point."

"And what is so special about those places?" Augusta brushed a strand of hair from her face.

"Well, Kissing Rock is a fascinating rock formation along Flirtation Walk, a popular walking path on the school grounds. Tradition says that a cadet must kiss his girl as they pass underneath the rock or it will fall, crushing both of them."

As he was explaining the custom, she slowly moved back so she could gently lean against a large rock.

"Is that a fact, Mr. Lewis?"

"It is." He placed a hand on the rock next to her and his other hand on her waist.

"I suppose we can pretend to be there. Make up for lost time. I think you should kiss me here and now." She touched his cheek and he bent and softly did so.

"I love you, Augusta." He pulled back and looked into her deep blue eyes. She smiled.

"I love you too, Michael." Her father's words about how she was supposed to end the courtship flashed through her mind, but she knew now that she would not do it. She could never let Michael go.

Other voices could be heard from down the pathway. Michael took her hand and continued walking.

"I'd like to come and visit you during one of my next leaves. I'm not sure when that will be, but I would like to speak with your father personally, about our marriage. Are you still agreeable to that?"

Augusta sighed. "I love you Michael, I truly do, and when I'm here with you, the answer is so simple." She stopped walking for a second and he led her to a nearby bench.

"I'd ask what your hesitation is, but that would be foolish. I know all the issues, but I think we can overcome them as long as we're together." He held her hands in his. "Which one makes you question the proposal the most?"

Augusta was silent for a moment. Michael's heart hammered, not wanting to pressure her too much, but anxious to hear her reply.

"I am afraid you'll think me terribly selfish." She finally responded softly.

"Being cautious and practical doesn't make one selfish," he replied, not surprised that she felt as she did.

"Well, for one thing, I'm concerned about your career." She placed a hand on his forearm. "Please hear me out. All my life, it has been impressed on me that I must marry well, someone with money and connections, someone who can keep me in the comforts I am used to."

Michael's heart sank. She wouldn't break off the courtship just because he wasn't as wealthy as she was? He hadn't misread her that much, had he?

"Michael, I want to say yes, truly, I do. To throw caution to the wind and marry you, follow you wherever you may be stationed, but alas, my father has made it clear that he wants more for me. He also insinuated, well...he told me that my mother would feel the same way."

Michael's heart sank even further. He couldn't fight that. She may be able to convince her father, but this loyalty to her mother would make things quite muddled.

"I want to marry you, Michael. I love you. I need you to know that, but with my father being against us and Andrew having his concerns. He worries about our future together because of the problems in our country. Please understand that I must heed their request or I may face the possibility of having to cut all ties with my family. And you, being a soldier, well, you know that isn't the safest profession. I would worry constantly about you, and if something did happen to you, where would I go? Besides, the last thing I would want is for you to feel as though you tore me away from my family, or for you to be saddled with a persnickety Southern wife who might make your life miserable."

"You could never make me feel that way, Augusta. If you were my wife, I would consider myself the luckiest man alive."

"You are the sweetest man I have ever met, Michael Lewis." She touched his cheek. "And that may be enough to make me believe that I can do this. That we can do this. There's just much for me to consider."

"I do understand your fears, Augusta. I must admit, I agree with your family that the country isn't solving any of the problems. We are likely headed for an armed conflict and that, unfortunately, is something to consider. However, I truly believe we can get through anything together." He paused and gently touched his lips to hers. "May I ask if you have prayed about this situation?"

She looked surprised. "Prayed? Why, Heavens no, I hadn't even considered that. It's just not something I was taught to do."

"Well, let me tell you, I have. That is why I know we can do this. We can overcome anything through Christ who gives us strength."

"My, that's quite poetic, Michael."

"Why, thank you lovely lady, but I can't take credit for it. It's from the letters of St. Paul."

"And thats..."

"In the Bible." He took a deep breath, new concerns rising. He knew the Byron family didn't attend church, but he thought she should at least know some of the more prominent verses.

"Oh." Augusta bit her lip. "I must confess, I've not read much of the Bible. I don't even think we have one at my house."

"Well," Michael decided to take a chance. "I have my Bible back in the barracks. You can take it with you, if you'd like. You can read through it and see the notes I've taken. It may actually help you decide what is planned for your future. I might also suggest you try praying. However you feel most comfortable. There's no wrong way to pray. Just talk with God and ask Him to help guide you."

"I suppose I can try that," Augusta replied. "If you think it will help. I would love to have the inner peace you always seem to have. Joseph told me once that it was your faith."

Michael's heart warmed at the knowledge that Augusta had discussed him with her brother. He knew Augusta was meant to be his wife. Now, he just had to convince her.

Part 3: 1859

Monday, July 6, 1859
Byron Hill Plantation
My dearest Augusta,

It is almost unbearable to me that I haven't seen you in over a year. I thank God every day that your father has allowed us to continue writing, for I would be miserable if I didn't have any contact with you. I hopefully will be granted a leave soon and will make visiting you my top priority.

I have been reassigned to Chicago, a rapidly growing city on the shores of Lake Michigan, in Illinois. It is believed that Chicago will be a gateway of trade to the western United States, and we are working to maximize the navigability of the river. It's quite difficult because of a large sandbar at the mouth of the Chicago River, where it meets Lake Michigan. I really enjoy the work, as it stimulates me both physically and mentally. I am very glad I was able to get assigned to the Corps of Engineers.

When not working or reading your letters, I am enjoying learning about and playing a new game, baseball, which has become quite popular. In fact, I heard that just yesterday, Amherst College and Williams College, both in Massachusetts, played the first ever intercollegiate baseball game. It will be interesting to see how the game develops over the next few years.

I haven't heard from Joseph in quite some time. I do hope he is faring well. I would like to hear if you have any news from him. I have noticed some increased tensions between soldiers from the South and the civilians and soldiers from the North. I am sad to say that I actually got involved in a fisticuffs and had to pull a soldier in my company off of another soldier. They were fighting, of course, about the state of our country. I fear we are on our way to a 'point of no return'. Despite that, I am still very earnest about my plans to marry you. I hope to convince your father of that sooner rather than later. I love you, Augusta, and nothing will change that.

I am very glad to hear that you continue to read the bible I loaned you and are praying more, as you stated in your last letter. I hope it gives you the comfort that it gives me.

You are constantly in my thoughts and prayers. I love you with all I have,

Michael.

"He asks about you." Augusta turned to Joseph, who had leave and was visiting the family. "Why don't you write him and tell him how you are doing?"

"For the same reason I rarely send you a letter. I'm not a writer, Augusta." He kicked his feet out and leaned against the backrest of the bench in the Byron Hill flower garden.

"And that's not something you could try and improve on?" She chided him.

"Perhaps, if I wanted to. I enjoy spending my free time playing baseball as well." He grinned saucily.

"Well, I'll just have to enjoy every moment with you while you're here, since I won't hear from you once you leave."

"Most probably," he replied. "So, when are you going to put my friend out of his misery and marry him? He's been sweet on you since the first day you met."

"Yes, I've gathered that." She sighed. "If it was just a matter of affection, Joseph, there would be no question of my marrying him, at least in my eyes. Besides you know full well my reasons for hesitating."

"No, I don't, please tell me," Joseph said. Augusta took a deep breath. She felt as though she were continually repeating herself in regards to her reasons for not saying 'yes' to Michael.

"Where do I start? Our backgrounds are very different. He's a northerner and the son of a shop owner. I'm a Southern girl who was raised on a plantation."

"I figured that was what you'd say," Joseph interrupted her, "and I'm telling you that's poppycock. You shouldn't let his finances or station in life deter you. Michael Lewis is one of the best men I know, and there is no one else on this earth that I would rather have my only sister marry, Yankee or not."

"Neither Father nor Andrew agree with you." Augusta felt tears welling up in her eyes.

"That's because they both think too much. Andrew gets that from Father. You and I, however, take after Mother. We let our hearts dictate our decisions, not our brains. At least, I thought you were more like that."

"How do you know that? About Mother, that is," Augusta asked. "You were only, what...four years old when she died. How can you even remember her?"

"I remember very little about Mother, but what I do remember is that she had a big heart. You do know that you were the only child in the family to have a wet nurse and nanny. Mother actually took care of Andrew and I. She went against what was socially acceptable because she wanted to spend all her time with us. That proved to me that she cared more about what felt right in her heart rather than what society expected."

Augusta bit her lip. "I suppose that makes sense."

"Not only that, Father once told me that I was more like Mother because I think with my heart and not my head. Granted, it wasn't a compliment at the time and he was using it as a criticism to me in one of his many lectures a few years back. But, because of this, I'm fairly confident that Mother would approve of you and Michael."

"That's not what Father said," Augusta told him.

"Well, it doesn't surprise me that he told you something different. Listen, Augusta, I love Father dearly, but he likes things his way. He will do just about anything, and usually at any cost to attain his goal, yet I believe in this instance he may just be lying to himself. Maybe he actually believes she would agree with him."

"Perhaps," Augusta replied.

"However, the way I see it, the choice is yours. You're twenty years old, and you're smart enough to make your own decisions. Father may protest and threaten, but it's all bluster when it comes to you. He loves you and I know he will not reject you even if you decide to marry Michael. Which, of course, I believe you should do."

"I don't recall you ever being this sentimental, Joseph." Augusta smiled and nudged his shoulder.

"Have you found a young lady that you'd like to impress in your travels out west?"

"Unfortunately, no." He gave her his most charming smile. "It will take a very special woman to get me to the altar. I'm not exactly sure what I'd even like to see in my future wife, but I feel as though I'll know her the first moment I meet her."

"That is actually quite sweet, Joseph Byron."

"I can be when I want to be." He nodded. "You really must think about what I told you though, in regards to Michael. You won't find anyone better than him."

"I have a feeling you're right." Augusta murmured.

Monday, October 19, 1859
Byron Hill Dining Room

"Letters from town, Mista Ian." One of the house slaves, Miles, brought the missives and Ian took them off the tray.

"Any for me, Father?" Augusta asked hopefully. She hadn't heard from Michael in over two months. She knew he was busy with his work, but this had been the longest she had gone without receiving news from him.

"No," he replied, reading the first letter, then the second one. He shook his head.

"What is it, Father?" Andrew asked.

"Robert E. Lee and the Virginia Militia put down an insurrection in Harpers Ferry that was instigated by that murderer, John Brown."

"Good. Were the lunatic or any of his sons killed?" Andrew took a bite of his eggs.

"No, but they were all captured and arrested. They should hang at least John Brown if there's any justice in the world," Ian replied.

"Surly you don't really feel that way, Father." Augusta was concerned about the vehemence in her father's tone. She had heard about the insurrection at Harpers Ferry and was so glad that Michael was no longer stationed there.

"I most certainly do, Augusta. That man had plans to rob a Federal armory. He was going to arm the slaves of Virginia and lead them into a bloody rebellion. They would have massacred any white man, woman or child they could find, and they wouldn't have stopped until we were all dead."

"That cannot possibly be true," Augusta protested.

"Sounds like you've been listening to Michael Lewis a bit too much," Andrew said dryly.

"No. Well, not about that at least. I haven't even heard from him in months," Augusta said. "I just can't imagine someone would do that."

"That's one of your problems, Augusta, you don't think with your head." Ian was trying to hold his temper. "You are too kind and you believe the best about everyone, but that's not always the case, especially in this instance. There is no good in that man." He stood and stomped to the buffet table to pour himself some water. "This is why I don't want you to marry a dang Yankee. I told you that you need to end the courtship, yet you disobeyed me."

Augusta gasped. "Father, I..."

"We are heading for war, Augusta, mark my words. We've had this discussion before, and I am darn tired of repeating myself. It's foolish for you and Michael Lewis to want to get married." He strode back to his seat and held up the other letter Miles had brought. "Which I intend to tell him when he comes to call."

"What?" Augusta's heart sped up. "When? He's here?"

"He's been assigned to Fort Sumter, he writes. He asked permission to call on you and would like to speak with me."

"And will you give him an answer? Father, what..."

"I'll listen to him and I'll allow you to see him, against my better judgment, but I will not give him permission to marry you."

"Father, please..." She had never seen her father so dead set against something.

"I'm sorry, Augusta, I just can't." Ian strode out of the dining room. Augusta stood to follow him, to try and reason with him, but Andrew grabbed her arm as she passed.

"Let him go. You'll only make him more angry and more unreasonable. I don't think you're persuasive way of talking will penetrate his brain just yet. Give him time to consider things, and let Michael speak with him as well." Augusta sat down.

"I hope Michael can talk some sense into Father, Andrew." Augusta said with tears in her eyes. "I can't tell you how much I need to be with Michael."

Later that Day

Michael practically skipped up the steps, glad that Ian Byron had responded to his request so quickly. Just as he was about to knock on the door, it opened and before he could get his bearings, Augusta squealed happily and threw herself into his arms.

"Oh, Michael. I am so glad you're here. I have missed you so."

His arms went around her in a hug and he closed his eyes. It felt good to have her in his embrace again. He pulled back slightly and kissed her gently on the lips.

"Not nearly as much as I've missed you, Augusta." She didn't seem to want to let him go. "We have so much to catch up on." She brushed a strand of hair off his forehead.

"I know, but isn't Father expecting you? I must caution you, though, he is going to make life quite difficult for us. He is angry right now with the political turmoil and that anger is centered on all of the Yankees."

Michael grimaced. "I suppose you've all heard about the Harpers Ferry incident." He shook his head. "Rotten timing for us."

"Well, if anyone can convince Father to change his mind, it's you." She kissed him again. "I'll be praying for you," she whispered. He smiled broadly.

"That thought encourages me more than you can imagine, but you're the sweet-talker in this relationship. I don't know if I'll be able to change his mind if you can't." He gave her another quick kiss before she took his hand and led him to her father's study.

"Father, Michael is here," she announced. Ian Byron looked up from the ledger he had been writing in, then stood.

"Michael, welcome. Augusta, please excuse us, and shut the door as you leave, please."

Augusta opened her mouth as if to say something, but thought better of it. She gave Michael an encouraging smile, then kissed his cheek and walked out the door, closing it behind her.

"You've won her heart, I will give you that." Ian gestured to the empty seat across his desk. Michael took it.

"No, sir, she has taken mine. Thank you for seeing me on such short notice. I am glad to be back in your beautiful home."

"Well, the tide has changed dramatically since the last time you were here," Ian replied.

"Yes, sir, that is true."

"We both know why you're here, Michael, so enough pleasantries. I assume you want to make an offer of marriage for Augusta."

"Yes, sir. I love Augusta with all my heart. I'd like your permission to ask for her hand in marriage."

"I'm sorry, I can't give it, and I won't insult your intelligence by explaining why."

"I understand that, Mr. Byron, I do. To be honest, if I were in your position, I might say the same thing. But I know, deep down, that Augusta and I are meant to be together, and I will do whatever I need to do to convince you of that."

"Does that include waiting until the problems of this country are solved?" Ian folded his hands on his desk.

"I think if you're honest with yourself, sir, you would realize that the problems we face today won't be resolved for decades. It has taken a hundred years for our country to get to this point and it may take that much time to resolve the problems. Now, I would wait that long for her, truly, I would. She is well worth waiting for, but I think it would be a bit unfair to the both of us."

Ian's jaw tightened. Michael's heart beat heavily. Mr. Byron's answer would affect the rest of his life. "At the very least, sir, please allow me to continue courting Augusta. I'm stationed at Fort Sumter, as you know. I'm not sure for how long, but I will have the ability to finally court her properly. At least give me a chance to change your mind."

"I suppose I can allow that," Ian replied after a long pause. "I'm not promising anything else, though."

"I understand, sir," Michael said, relieved that he at least had the opportunity to court the love of his life.

Augusta stood as she saw Michael walk around the corner of the house and into her favorite garden. His face was difficult to read. They hurried towards each other and she threw herself into his arms. "Please tell me he said yes," she murmured.

"Not exactly." Michael pulled away. "He refused permission for me to marry you, but I was able to convince him to allow me to continue courting you."

"Well, that is at least promising, though I was hoping for a miracle in him allowing us to marry as soon as possible."

"It's good to hear that you believe in miracles." He smiled.

"You have convinced me, I must admit. I do have a lot of questions and thoughts to work through, but I think I'm on my way."

"I am so, undeniably glad to hear that." He brought her hands to his lips, kissed them, and smiled. "Your father did invite me to dinner tonight, which again, is promising, but I had to decline. I must get back to my post soon. I had the opportunity to get away and I needed to see you, even if only for a short time."

"I'm so happy you did." She squeezed his hand. "And it is so fortuitous to have you in Charleston. I suppose when you have the skills and abilities that you do, you get your choice of placements."

"I did have some say in my assignment, I suppose." He smiled. "And I will visit whenever and as often as I can. It may be on short notice, or no notice at all. We must somehow convince your father that he needs to change his mind in regards to our marriage."

Augusta leaned over and kissed him on the cheek. "I believe you are right."

Wednesday, November 4, 1859
Byron Hill Plantation

The weeks dragged on for Augusta. Having Michael so close to her, yet unable to see him whenever she wanted was almost worse than him being in a different state. She had only been able to see him about once a week, usually on Sundays, in church. Sunday church services were very important to him and she didn't mind going as much as she thought she would, especially since it gave her the opportunity to spend time with Michael.

Augusta sat in the parlor on this afternoon. It was a dreary day so far, both in terms of weather and the mood of the house. Her father had been surly, even more so lately, and Augusta wondered how much longer they could be at this stalemate with her impatiently waiting for Ian to give his permission to marry Michael. Unfortunately, the waiting had a way of making Augusta's own doubts rise up again. She had been encouraged by what Joseph had said about their mother, but her father insisted that Kayleen Byron would have wanted her daughter to make a societal match. Augusta didn't know who to believe.

"I thought you might be in here." Andrew entered the room, looking the perfect gentleman, as always.

"What is it you need, Andrew?" She set down the novel she had been reading. Her brother sat on the settee next to her, a leather-bound book in his hands.

"I have gone back and forth about giving you this."
He leaned forward, his elbows on his knees.
"However, I believe that it will be best for everyone if
I do." He took a deep breath. "I personally don't
want you to marry a Yankee, yet I want you to be
happy. It's become quite obvious that those two
things seem to be in opposition."

"They are," Augusta replied. "I know it's hard for
you and Father to believe, but I love Michael and the
two of us becoming man and wife will bring me all
the joy I need." She looked at her brother. "There are
days when I wish I'd never fallen in love with
Michael, knowing it would make my life easier right
now, but he brings me only happiness. We were
meant to be. I can't imagine my life without him,
Andrew."

"Yes, I've come to understand that." Andrew
handed her the book. "Which is why I am giving you
this."

"Wherever did you get it?"

Andrew blushed. "Mother gave it to me. Right
before she died. You'd already been born, and Joseph
and I were able to visit her. I'm not sure if she knew
she was going to die, but she gave me the book and
asked me to share it with you and Joseph when you
were older. I must admit, I've been selfish, hoarding
this last piece of her to myself."

Augusta could feel her heart racing, excited about
the prospect of getting to know her mother through

the diary. A sense of longing welled up in her. "Oh, thank you, Andrew."

"I should have given it to you years ago. Then you would have realized...all she wanted was for her children to be happy and healthy. Honestly, she would have probably approved of Michael, though it pains me to admit that."

Augusta fingered the pages, emotionally thinking about the mother she never had a chance to meet. "I can't wait to read it."

"Well, I'll allow you to start now, then." Andrew stood. Augusta did so as well and gave him a tight hug.

"I love you, Andrew," she said.

"I love you too, Augusta."

Part 4: 1860

Friday, May 18, 1860
Byron Hill

"Azalea Harris! What brings you all the way out here?" Augusta smiled at her friend as she entered the parlor.

"I just realized it's been months since we've had a proper visit," Azalea replied.

That's true enough," Augusta said, "let me ring for tea."

"No please don't bother." Azalea held up a hand. "I don't wish to interrupt any of your people in what they are currently doing."

"Of course." Augusta sometimes forgot that Azalea was very much in opposition to slavery. "Is there any important news from town?"

"The new Republican party has selected Abraham Lincoln as their candidate for presidency."

"And I can bet that you and the rest of your blasted abolitionists just love that." Andrew strode into the room, an angry look on his usually calm face. Augusta sighed. Andrew and Azalea never got along. Augusta wasn't sure why. Perhaps it was only their political beliefs, but she felt it went deeper than that. Someday, she would learn the real reason.

"As a matter of fact, Mr. Byron, I would not support Mr. Lincoln even if I could vote. He doesn't want to abolish slavery if he's elected. It's said that he'll allow slavery to continue in the southern states. That should make you and the other slavers happy."

"For a man like him to be in office? Hardly. The fact that he won't allow slavery into new territories is an economic and political threat to all southerners."

"Not all southerners, Mr. Byron, just those who feel the need to profit from the sweat of their slaves." Azalea's voice rose as she stood.

Augusta wanted to melt back into the settee. She hated arguments and did whatever she could to avoid them.

"You abolitionists don't know what you're talking about! Freeing the slaves will only cause problems you're not ready to address!" Andrew took two steps forward, bringing him closer to Azalea. She closed the gap, as if to prove to him that she would not back down.

"You're holding your fellow human beings as property! Even a nonbeliever like you should see that's a barbaric practice."

"And you think just setting them free, unskilled and uneducated, to go out into the world, is the right thing to do?"

"At least they'd have a choice and not be subject to beatings anytime an overseer or master felt like it."

"How many years have you been coming out to Byron Hill? Have you ever, in all that time seen a slave mistreated here?"

"Augusta lives here and I doubt she's even seen anything of how a plantation is truly run. Men like you, Andrew, know how to hide all the little details." Azalea retorted.

"How dare you insinuate that? I'll have you know that Father prides himself on treating our slaves well."

"I don't believe that's even a possibility," Azalea snapped. "You and your desire to keep your free labor is going to pull us into a war, you mark my words."

"You abolitionists electing Lincoln is what will pull us into a war. The south won't stand for that man in the White House." He turned to Augusta, his voice softened. "In fact, that's what I was coming to talk with you about. I know we've spoken about your possible marriage to Michael Lewis. With this news, however, well, you need to realize what that means. If Lincoln is elected as President, the Southern States will probably try to secede again, South Carolina leading the way as usual."

"Yes, because if the southern planters can't win an election through the proper channels, they'll cry and stomp their feet for not getting their way."

Andrew turned back to Azalea, a deadly look on his face. "Do you ever stop harping?"

"Not if I have just cause," she replied, then sat back down and turned her back on Andrew.

"You need to consider the situation, Augusta," Andrew told his sister. "I don't want you to be hurt. It might not be in your best interest to marry him now." He then turned and walked out of the parlor.

"I desperately hope you don't listen to him." Azalea spoke to Augusta. "If you truly love Mr. Lewis, you should still marry him"

"That is what I intend to do," Augusta replied. "Though all this news about Lincoln won't make it any easier, especially with my father."

"You're old enough to make your own decisions, Augusta. If your father doesn't allow the marriage, you simply, tell him you're going to run away with the man you love."

"Michael loves me, but unfortunately, he would never do that. He is an honorable man and wants to do everything properly."

"So he's proper to a fault, just like your brother." Azalea didn't bother to hide the disdain in her voice.

"I don't believe there is anyone else as proper as Andrew." Augusta laughed. "I just know that he is so considerate that he wouldn't want to permanently damage the relationship I have with my family."

"If you marry Michael and your family disowns you, that's their loss. Besides, if I could find a man that loves me the way Michael evidently loves you, there is nothing on earth that would keep me from him."

Augusta bit her lip.

"Could you live without being married to Michael Lewis?" Azalea asked.

"I don't think so, no." Augusta responded honestly. "Not happily, at least."

"Then tell your father that and don't take 'no' for an answer."

"Azalea, there's no possible chance of me doing that. I'm nowhere near as assertive as you, and I don't like arguing."

"If you want to be with Michael, you must be strong, and never be afraid."

"I suppose so," Augusta replied meekly. "As Michael always says, 'God will be with us'."

"And that is exactly true. This Michael, he is a smart man. I wouldn't want to lose him if I were you. Although, if you do, perhaps I will snatch him up for myself."

Augusta snorted and took a deep breath. "All right, you convinced me. I'll speak with Father."

"Good," Azalea smiled. "I am positive you won't regret it."

Emboldened by Azalea's words, Augusta went into her father's office as soon as her friend left. She knew she had to petition Ian for his blessing on her marriage to Michael before she lost her nerve. She knew she didn't need his permission, but she loved her father dearly and desperately wanted his approval.

"Father, may I speak with you?" She asked. He nodded grimly, as if he knew what she was there for.

"You are always welcome in here, Augusta, no matter what, you know that."

"That's good of you to remind me, especially in regards to what I want to talk with you about."

"You've made a decision regarding Michael Lewis, I assume."

"My decision in regards to Michael has been made for quite some time, Father. I love him and I want to marry him. I just can't live without him, Father."

"You realize your mother…"

"You cannot try and tell me that, Father. Andrew gave me Mother's journal. I believe she would like Michael, and I am not happy that you all but lied to me."

Ian's expression tightened. "That may be true. Perhaps I should have been more upfront with you. I must ask, though, what if I told you 'no' yet again?" Ian folded his hands on the desk. Augusta, feeling suddenly confident in her beliefs, stood straight and tall.

"You know I love you too, Father, but if you are to deny me yet again, I will go against your wishes and marry Michael without your blessing, though I really prefer it not to be that way."

"Would Michael agree to this? He doesn't strike me as the kind of man who would go against protocol."

"You are correct in thinking that, Father, but I am confident in my ability to convince him otherwise."

"You're serious, aren't you? You realize that we could go to war with the Yankees." He reminded her yet again. "If you go north, you will be considered the enemy. The two of you will be constantly harassed from both sides. Michael would be fighting against your family and friends."

"I am aware of that. Father, we know what we're facing, both in the north and the south. We know it will be difficult, we can't pretend it will be easy, but we love each other. We want to be together, especially if the war will eventually separate us, and we pray to God that will never happen. Father, I'm not a little girl any more. This is what I want, no, this is what I must do with my life."

"You're sure?"

Hope welled up in Augusta's heart. Her father wasn't putting up as much of an argument as in the past. Could he have changed his mind? "Yes, Father. I've never been so sure about anything in my life."

Her father clenched his jaw and didn't speak for what felt like an hour. Finally, he nodded. "All right then, I still have my doubts, I don't believe this is what's best for you, and I do not approve. I will not give you formal permission to marry Michael, but I will give you my blessing."

"Oh, thank you, Father!" She exclaimed, springing from her chair and rushing around the desk to hug him.

"I love you Augusta, and I sincerely hope he makes you happy." Ian hugged her tightly and dropped a kiss on the top of her head.

"I love you too." She pulled back from the embrace. "Can we have one of the men go into town with a message for Michael so I can tell him the news?"

"I have some errands I must run in Charleston. If you'd like, you can come with me and we can both tell him the news. Is there a day that will be too soon for your wedding? What must you plan?"

"I could be ready as soon as tomorrow if we can get the church." Augusta clapped her hands.

"The church." Ian grunted. "Michael's church?"

"Yes, Father, St. Mary of the Annunciation. My church of late as well."

"I was so caught up with the fact that he's a Yankee that I forgot he's also a Papist." Ian sighed. "Well, your mother's sister married a Catholic and the world didn't end."

"Oh, Father, don't be silly, what does it really matter to you anyway? We all believe in the same God." Augusta assured him.

"We'll leave after lunch, then." Ian pulled his jacket on. "Hopefully we will be able to see your intended."

Wednesday, May 23, 1860
Byron Hill Plantation

"I am so glad you are able to stand up with me." Augusta smiled at Azalea as Emmy fixed her hair. She hadn't seen Michael since her father gave his blessing. He was unable to get any time away, but they had corresponded frequently through messages. Augusta had sent a message to Joseph, but no one knew if he would receive it in time or get the leave necessary to come to the wedding.

Michael had sent a message to his parents, but they would not be able to make it to South Carolina on such short notice. Augusta had suggested spending their wedding trip in Pennsylvania. Michael had been given a fourteen day leave starting with their wedding day, which would be just enough time for the trip. She wondered if they could have a reception in Gettysburg so she could meet the friends and family that he grew up with.

"I'm honored that you asked me," Azalea said.

"You are very dear to me," Augusta replied. "You have stood by me through much, the betrayal of Jeffrey and Margaret, the years of courting Michael, and I feel you may be the only person in South Carolina that truly supports Michael and me."

"Which to me is a tragedy," Azalea huffed. "You make such a fine couple, although knowing your brother Andrew, I shouldn't be surprised that he would be one of those against the two of you. He can be such a bully."

"Father and Andrew are just concerned about my happiness. Joseph has some misgivings, but he has always been supportive of the two of us,"

"That must be why I like Joseph better," Azalea commented.

"Well, I definitely have to say, it's like sparks and gunpowder when you and Andrew are around one another."

"I promise I will try to avoid him today, even though it will be a small reception and I may not be able to do so." Azalea smiled at her friend. "For you, however, I will hold my temper."

"Thank you for that," Augusta replied. Emmy put the finishing touches on Augusta's hair.

"Ya look just beautiful, Miz Augusta." Emmy stepped back to admire her work. Augusta stood. There hadn't been time for a dress to be made specifically for the wedding, but she had decided on a white ball gown with dark blue trim across the neckline and waist, and dark blue bows winding along the hemline.

"Thank you, Emmy." Augusta turned and took the woman's hands in hers. "I will miss you dreadfully."

"Oh, Miz Augusta, ya know ya can always come see me."

"I had assumed you would take Emmy with you to Charleston," Azalea said dryly.

"Oh, I've thought about it, that's for sure," Augusta said, "but there are some pressing reasons why I'd like her to stay here."

"Her daddy say I could stay as a housemaid and help when da family is entertainin'," Emmy explained. "Miz Augusta didn't want ta take me away from Stephen. He's my fellow."

"How considerate," Azalea replied. "It's too bad your father didn't gift her to you, Augusta. Then you would have the right to set her free if you chose to."

"Azalea..." Augusta's tone held warning.

"My mama, daddy, brother and fellow all lives here, Miz Azalea. Whatever I do with freedom?"

Azalea was just about to speak again, but saw Augusta's distressed look. "As much as I'd like to explain things to you, Emmy, it's Augusta's special day. I've probably already said too much."

"Thank you, Azalea. I realize how much passion you have for your cause, and I admire you for it, but I'd like to have a peaceful wedding."

"I'll do my best, as I said," Azalea replied.

There was a knock on the door and Dianna entered. "So sorry I havna been in here, I been makin sure everything be set and ready fo' ya reception. The ballroom looks beautiful an we have lanterns set up all around ya garden fo evening strolls." She took Augusta's forearms in her hands and looked her up and down, tears in her eyes. "Ya looks beautiful, child. Jus beautiful. Yo Mama would be so very proud of ya." She wiped a tear from her eye. "Ya been like my own child in many ways. I raised ya since yo poor Mama died. Ya remember now, if ya have any questions 'bout bein a married woman, ya just ask me any time."

"Thank you," Augusta replied. "I will keep that in mind." She hugged Dianna. "Thank you so much for everything."

"O' course, child." Dianna held her tightly for a moment, then gave her a pat on the back. "Let's get ya to da church!"

The wedding ceremony at the church was a blur to Augusta. She was amazed that she didn't cry, mainly because from the moment she started to walk down the aisle, Michael's eyes hadn't left hers. Augusta felt mesmerized and every time their eyes met during the ceremony, she seemed to fall more deeply in love with him. Augusta's decision to marry Michael was solidified. He looked so handsome in his Army dress uniform.

The small group returned to Byron Hill after the ceremony. As Dianna had said, the ballroom and gardens surrounding the plantation house had been turned into a beautiful reception area. The dinner and dance was a small gathering of friends and family who were able to attend on such short notice.

"I must say, you look absolutely radiant, my dear." Her father came up to her and hugged her.

"You've told me that already, Father. Several times, as a matter of fact." she replied.

"Yes, well I must say it again. You look so much like your mother." He had tears in his eyes, which caused Augusta to tear up as well,

"I wish she could be here today," Augusta said quietly.

"She's with us," he responded, and touched his heart. "She's always with us here."

Augusta nodded and hugged her father. "I love you, Father."

"I have only wanted what is best for you," he said.

"I know," she replied.

Augusta's Aunt Beverly from Charleston interrupted the sentimental conversation and gave her niece an embrace.

"My dear, I am so glad I was able to make the wedding! There was very little warning and no formal announcement made." Beverly was the wife of Ian Byron's brother, and she constantly worried about following the rules of social propriety.

"I'm quite sorry, Aunt Beverly. I wish I could have given more warning, but with the state of the country, we felt it best to get married sooner rather than later."

"I suppose that makes sense, but still, I wish you would have consulted me." Beverly sighed and fanned herself. "And where is your new husband? I have yet to meet him."

"He went for some lemonade and barbecue. I am famished," she replied.

"Attentive. That is a good quality in a husband." Beverly nodded her approval.

"Yes, he is quite attentive and caring." Augusta assured her aunt.

"Did the Yankee army give him sufficient time for a wedding trip?"

"Yes, they gave him two weeks. We're traveling to Pennsylvania to see his family. It will be the first time I meet his mother."

"Two weeks? Goodness, it should be three months or more." Beverly looked up as Michael approached, a plate and glass in his hand.

"Here you are, Mrs. Lewis." He smiled broadly at her as she took the glass from him.

"I like being called that." Augusta took a drink of the lemonade. "Michael, I would like you to meet my aunt, Beverly Byron, out of Charleston."

"It is a pleasure to meet you, Mrs. Byron." He bowed slightly.

"Good Heavens, boy, call me Aunt Beverly. Whether we like it or not, you're a part of the family now.

"Thank you, Ma'am."

"Beverly is also Azalea's aunt. Azalea's mother was Beverly's sister."

"Yes, God rest her soul. My sister is likely turning over in her grave at the knowledge of how that girl has turned out. The Lord knows I tried to rein her in and turn her into a proper Southern lady, but to no avail. Mark my words, our Azalea will die a pitiful, if spirited, spinster."

"Thank you so much for saying so, Aunt Beverly. I am glad to know what you truly think of me." Azalea approached the small group.

"You cannot be surprised to hear me say that, niece. I say the same thing to you all the time. You know how I feel."

"That is true, Aunt Beverly. Everyone knows how you feel." Azalea looked as though she wanted to argue more, but she refrained, likely remembering her promise to Augusta.

"I, for one, am very grateful for Miss Harris." Michael spoke up. "I know through my correspondence with Augusta these last few years that her friendship has been invaluable to my wife." He gave Azalea a comforting smile.

"She has indeed, Aunt Beverly." Augusta spoke up. "In fact, had Azalea not encouraged me, I may have never pushed Father to accept Michael's offer."

"I see." Beverly's expression made it appear as though she had just sucked on a fresh lemon. "At any rate, I do hope you have a splendid wedding trip, despite it's short length, my dear. Please come for a visit when you return. I assume you'll be staying in town, correct?"

"Yes. Michael will rent a room," Augusta replied. "I look forward to the opportunity of frequently visiting family and friends in Charleston." She smiled at Azalea. "It will be a nice change."

Thursday, June 7, 1860
Streets of Charleston

The wedding trip was over before Augusta had time to think. They were never able to make it to Gettysburg, as moments before they left Charleston, Michael had been given army dispatches to take to Washington City, then additional papers to deliver in Philadelphia. Luckily, the newlyweds had gotten word to Samuel and Aideen who were able to make travel arrangements to Philadelphia, so Augusta finally had the opportunity to meet her mother-in-law. Augusta immediately liked the kind, motherly woman, a short, stout redhead. Aideen had made her feel like a welcomed family member from the first introductions and insisted that Augusta call her 'Mother'.

Augusta and Michael had returned to Charleston and were settling into a quiet routine. Today Augusta had been out running some errands and was returning home when she looked down the street. "Oh, botheration," Augusta muttered as she saw Margaret Wiggs-Cullen approach her, flanked by two other socialites that Augusta had never really cared for, Romilda Wilson and Dorothy Abernathy. Augusta glanced around, but there was no way to avoid the trio.

"My, my, if it isn't the Yankee-lover. My goodness, Augusta, how can you even show your face here in Charleston after what you have done?" Margaret smirked.

"Mrs. Cullen, I am sorry you feel that way, but in all honesty, I don't feel you have any right to speak in such a way, after what you did to me." Augusta hated confrontation, and hoped she could avoid it here. "Now, if you'll just let me pass, I won't bother you anymore."

"Oh, you'll bother me, simply by living here in Charleston, married to the enemy. Why, if that Yankee had his way, none of us would be able to keep our people, and our way of life would be topsy-turvy. You do realize, dear Augusta, that if the ape, Lincoln, is elected, you and your husband best be on the first train out of town. I wouldn't want any retaliation putting either one of you in harm's way. I can't imagine why you would even want to stay here once the war starts. Why, if a Confederate were to fall in battle, I dread to think of what may happen to the mistress of a Yankee officer."

Augusta's face reddened. She wasn't sure how to respond, so she simply tried to step onto the street so she could be on her way. Before she took that step, however, a familiar voice stopped her.

"Margaret Cullen, how dare you!" Azalea Harris stepped next to Augusta and slipped an arm through her friend's in a show of support. "Augusta does not deserve any harsh words from you. If I didn't know any better, I would think you were jealous. Augusta has a kind, successful man for her husband, a man who will be brave enough to fight for his country and his beliefs, while your husband has already been heard to say that he plans on avoiding service to the South."

"Well at least Margaret has a husband, Azalea Harris," Romilda Wilson taunted. "We all know you'll never find one."

Augusta felt the need to defend Azalea. "That's unfair of you to say, Mrs. Wilson. Azalea will find the man that compliments her beliefs and he will make her happy, unlike you and your marriage."

"If I do get married, you can bet it will be a match like Augusta's, not like any of yours. I prefer a man that will care about me and not just my dowry." Azalea's words were cool and calm.

"As if any decent man will want you anyways," Dorothy said. "Everyone knows you would just as soon set all the slaves free. It's unpatriotic. And to think two of your brothers agree with you. Mason Harris is your only brother who is on the right side."

"Well, then, I suppose it's a good thing that none of my brothers ever tried to court you, Miss Abernathy, though it was never for lack of effort on your part." Azalea smirked.

"Why, I never!" Dorothy sputtered.

"Come along, ladies." Margaret had apparently had enough. "We shouldn't be seen talking to either of these women. Folks may believe we're actually friends, and I don't wish to have that association."

Once the women passed, Margaret turned back and spoke with a smile. "You must remember what I said, Augusta. If Lincoln is elected, you'd best move on."

"Oh, if I weren't concerned with being a lady..." Azalea growled. "I do hope you don't put any stock into what that miserable woman says."

"I don't, not anymore," Augusta assured her. "Although I feel more hurt, as well as foolish, that I once considered her to be one of my best friends."

"Don't concern yourself, Augusta. You know, I believe Margaret would be very successful on the stage. She excels at allowing people to see only what she wants them to see. Unlike me." She grinned sheepishly.

"Well, I must say, I much prefer your friendship," Augusta said, then smiled brightly when she saw her husband striding toward them.

"Miss Harris." Michael was glad to see his wife speaking with Azalea, as he knew how much Augusta valued her friendship and he quite enjoyed her forward personality. "It is very good to see you. How is your father?"

"Quite well, with the exception of losing some business due to the narrow-minded people who live in this fine city not agreeing with his politics." She waved her hand in the air.

"Unfortunately, that may get worse as time goes on," Michael said.

"Yes, well, I am glad we can count on you to shop at our apothecary," she said brightly.

"Not for long, unfortunately." Michael ran a hand through his hair. A local man passed by and gave him a very unpleasant look. He tried to ignore it. Those looks had been present since he arrived in Charleston, but were becoming more frequent and tempestuous since returning from Pennsylvania. He looked at Augusta. "Which is what I must speak with you about, dear. I have been given new orders."

"Goodness, that sounds ominous." Augusta looked concerned.

"Well then, I'll leave you to it." Azalea nodded at the two and went in the direction of one of her father's shops. Michael took Augusta's arm and began leading her back towards their boardinghouse.

"So, what are your new orders?" Augusta braved the question.

"I am to leave for Washington City on Saturday," he replied. "You can come with me, and I would like you to do so, but it must be your decision."

"There is no other choice for me. Where you go I will go, and where you stay I will stay. Your people will be my people and your God my God. As long as it's allowed, of course."

He smiled. "You've been reading the Bible in your free time, I see."

"Yes, I find the book of Ruth very comforting."

He squeezed her arm. "I hoped you would."

"So I have two days to ready myself for the move." Augusta thought hard about what she should bring. "It won't be like it is now, where I can go home whenever I choose and pick up whatever I feel I may need."

"No, indeed not. Also, you will be limited to two trunks." Michael told her.

"Dear me." Augusta bit her lip.

As they turned a corner, a well-dressed civilian bumped into Michael.

"Excuse me," Michael said. The civilian looked at Michael, then gave him a shove when he saw Michael wore a Union uniform.

"Watch where you're going, bluebelly."

"Tom?" Augusta recognized the man. "Thomas McHenry, I know your mother raised you to be more of a gentleman than that."

"Augusta Byron?" The young man's eyes widened. "What is a proper Southern lady like yourself doing on the arm of Yankee trash like this?"

"He's my husband, Tom. I'm Mrs. Michael Lewis now." Augusta spoke sternly. The man's jaw dropped.

"What was your father thinking, allowing you to marry a Yankee soldier?" Thomas turned towards

Michael. "And who do you think you are, daring to even touch a Southern born girl? You should be run out of town on a rail for being with her." He shoved Michael again, who stumbled back a step and tried to hold his temper.

"Sir, just let us pass," Michael said, gently putting Augusta behind him.

"And you, Augusta, how could you sully yourself and your good name by marrying Yankee scum? I'd expect that from a harridan like Azalea Harris, but never you."

"Now, see here..." Michael tried to remain calm, but Thomas's next words were too vile and explicit against Augusta's moral character. Michael snapped. As Augusta gasped in embarrassment at the words, Michael clenched his jaw and stood face to face with Thomas McHenry.

"I would advise you to retract that statement and apologize to my wife, sir."

When Thomas's reply was even more filthy, Michael's temper flared. He threw a fist into Thomas's stomach, then into his face and the man crumpled to the ground. Michael knelt down and grabbed Thomas by the scruff of the neck. "Say what you will about me, but never insult my wife again. Do I make myself clear?" He shoved Tom down as he stood, shook his throbbing hand, and turned to Augusta. He couldn't tell if her look was of admiration or disgust, but she was certainly shocked by his actions.

"I am sorry you had to witness that, my love. Shall we continue on our way?"

"Yes, sir." The two stepped around Thomas McHenry, who was rubbing his jaw and glaring at the couple.

As they walked away, Michael bent down and whispered, "I truly am sorry you had to see that, Augusta. I may be a trained soldier, but I don't particularly care for violence."

"I must say, I was stunned that you actually hit him, but it is comforting to know that my kind, gentle husband can and will defend me if the need arises."

"Yes, I can and I will. I will defend you to my death."

Tuesday, November 6, 1860
Washington City

The months flew by for Augusta. She was introduced to several of the officers Michael worked with and their wives. She spent much of her time visiting with these women who weren't bothered by the fact that she was a Southerner. She had adjusted to not having servants and enjoyed a new sense of independence. Augusta spent the rest of her time reading and exploring the growing city of Washington. She especially liked to watch the progress on the construction of the new capitol building. It fascinated her to see such an achievement. However, spending as much time as she could with Michael was her priority. She knew it was only a matter of time before he would be taken from her.

Augusta was walking down Maryland Avenue, running some errands before she met Michael for lunch when she heard a familiar female voice greet her.

"Mrs. Lewis!" Augusta turned and smiled as Mrs. Rose Greenhow approached her. Mrs. Greenhow was from the south as well, Maryland, so Augusta felt a special friendship with her. The woman was a widow with four lovely daughters. Her late husband had worked with the State Department and she was very popular with the social and political leaders of Washington.

"Mrs. Greenhow, it is so nice to see you. I trust you're well?"

"Indeed. I just received a letter from my dear Florence. I desperately miss her." Florence Moore was Mrs. Greenhow's oldest daughter, who was also married to an army officer that graduated from West Point. The couple now resided in Ohio.

"I understand the heartache of being separated from one's family," Augusta said. The last six months living in Washington had made her appreciate her home so much more, and of course, the cooler temperatures made her long for the Carolina climate.

"Of course you do, my dear," Mrs. Greenhow patted her arm. "What brings you out on this chilly day?"

"I was running some errands, but Michael will be meeting me at Maryland Avenue and South Capitol Street. We're going to have lunch together."

"Well, hopefully, that handsome young husband of yours will meet you soon. This town is bound to go a little crazy once the election results start coming in."

"It's hard to avoid the fact that it is election day. I do wish we could vote as well," Augusta said, looking around the busy streets. "And I do hope there is no violence."

"I'd be surprised if there isn't," Mrs. Greenhow replied. "Some men need very little encouragement to cause a ruckus.

"That is true," Augusta said, then looked around to see Michael approaching them.

"Good day, my love." He took his wife's hands in his own. "Mrs. Greenhow, a pleasure to see you."

"Lieutenant Lewis. Were you able to cast your vote today?

"I was indeed. It is terribly busy at the polls, that's for sure." He glanced down the road. "Alas, I fear there may be some rioting if the election goes a certain way. Both of you women, well...you should definitely be off the streets. Augusta, I will escort you to the apartment after lunch. Mrs. Greenhow, may I have the pleasure of escorting you to your home also?"

"No, no, don't you worry about me, Lieutenant. I am quite capable of getting home myself. I hope to see the both of you later." Rose nodded and went toward her own home.

"It's going to get bad, isn't it?" Augusta leaned toward Michael, kissed his cheek, then took his arm.

"I'm afraid so, which is why, I don't want to take any chances. I don't want you on the streets when the presidency is announced." He pulled her tightly to his side as they began walking.

"I understand. I don't want my husband on the streets either, not if it's going to be dangerous."

"I know, unfortunately, that is part of my job right now."

"It doesn't make it easier for me to accept." Augusta sighed. The hotel they were to dine at came into view, and they walked in silence for a moment. "What do you think will happen if Lincoln is elected?" She finally asked.

"I believe Lincoln is the best choice of the four candidates, but I've heard reports that the Southern states are afraid that the existence of slavery is at stake and that if he is elected, South Carolina, Mississippi, Alabama, Georgia and Florida will break away and form their own country."

"And that's what will start a war," Augusta said quietly. They walked up the steps to the hotel and into the dining room for lunch.

"I'm afraid so," Michael replied, "though I hear it's the last thing that Lincoln wants. He wants peace and unity."

"And yet, that will not be the case." Augusta sat down and Michael pushed her chair in.

"Unfortunately, you are right." Michael sat across from her. "Those Southern states have made it clear." The two ordered their meals, and Michael reached across the table to take one of Augusta's hands in his. "I can dine with you, but after I escort you home, I must get back to my post. I understand it may be tiresome, all alone in our small apartment, but I will feel much better if I know where you are and that you are safe."

"I suppose I can write some letters to Father, Azalea and Aunt Bernice, and Joseph, of course. I've been a bit remiss in that department."

"I do wish Joseph would write one of us. I really would like to see him, talk with him. I fear..." Michael paused. Augusta squeezed his hand as their food arrived. "I'm afraid he's going to leave the Union Army and end our friendship."

"He may fight for the south, Michael, but I'm certain he will always consider you a friend." Augusta reassured him.

"I hope so. With the exception of you, Joseph is the best friend I've ever had."

"I know Joseph well. He's loyal to those he cares about. He values your friendship as much as you do."

"Thank you for saying so. I'm nervous about this war for many reasons, but my biggest fear is that it will tear families like yours apart."

"Well, we'll just have to pray that a war never comes to fruition and if it does, we will work extremely hard to keep our family together."

Thursday, December 20, 1860
Corps of Engineers Headquarters-Washington City

"Well, they've done it."

"Michael glanced up from the report he was writing and looked at his fellow officer, Gerald Mason.

"Secession?" Michael asked.

"Yes, blast it." Mason slammed the report on his desk. "Those South Carolina firebrands have announced that the union that exists between South Carolina and other states in the Union is hereby dissolved." He let out a stream of cursing. "They're demanding that all property held by the Federal government must be abandoned."

"Like Sumter and Moultrie?" Michael hadn't wanted to take Augusta from her family, but with this news, he was glad he had been transferred. South Carolina, especially Charleston, would be a powder keg waiting to explode.

"Yes, and if we don't withdraw, they claim it will justify them in using deadly force." Mason shook his head. "A blasted mess."

"That's when the first shots of the war will be fired, mark my words." Michael shook his head.

"Probably." Mason took a cigar out of his shirt pocket, then cut it and lit it. "You have kin in the south, don't you, Lewis?"

"My wife is from South Carolina, actually. She's here in Washington with me, but her father and one of her brothers own a plantation near Charleston. Her other brother is in the Union Army, Lieutenant Joseph Byron. He graduated with me from the Point, and he's stationed in Texas right now, at least, he was when we last heard from him."

"Not sure how you or anyone can admit to being friendly with anyone from South Carolina. They're about to tear our country apart."

"There are many Southerners who don't want to go to war, Mason. Even if they choose to fight against us. It's the hotheads causing the turmoil."

"Well, either way, it won't be a problem. We'll destroy any army they raise in weeks."

"I wouldn't be so sure about that." Michael thought about some of the Southerners he knew. Men like Andrew Byron and his father, who weren't trained as soldiers, but had been raised on horseback and hard work. They would likely take to soldiering rather quickly and easily.

"We have superior numbers in our ranks, Lewis, as well as the fact that we are in the right. States cannot leave the Union whenever they want. It's unconstitutional. This is a union."

"I agree with you, Mason. My ancestors fought for this Union in multiple wars, and I'll gladly fight to keep it from being torn apart."

"That's good to know. I wouldn't think you'd be the type to hide behind your wife's Southern skirts." He shook his head. "Though I still find it hard to believe your wife is a rebel. Was it an arranged marriage or some such thing?"

"Not at all."

"Well, I may have misjudged you, Lewis. I would have thought you had better judgment in women."

Michael was irritated. Mason hadn't even met Augusta. "I do and she is quite possibly the finest woman in Washington right now, Mason." Michael tucked the papers he was working on in a folder and stood. "There is no one I would rather share my life with, and you should meet her before you make a judgement."

"Well, maybe so, but the war is coming and men will be killed. You plan on leaving her here all alone in Washington? That's asking for trouble if you know what I mean. The daughter of our enemy, in the nation's capital, all on her lonesome, and what if you don't come back from the war."

Michael looked at the man, shocked. "Are you threatening me or my wife in some way, Mason?"

"Not at all, Lewis, not at all. I'm merely suggesting that you may want to consider the ramifications of leaving a Southern woman alone in the capitol. Where will your little rebel stay once you are transferred to active duty?"

Michael had been thinking about this very scenario ever since Lincoln had been elected, but he still hadn't made a decision.

Mason continued. "Some women will likely follow their men around from camp to camp. Maybe she could do that. From what you say, she would certainly be nice to have around. To look at, that is."

"Mason, are you trying to rile me up?"

"Not at all, my man, not at all." Mason smiled rakishly. "Just giving you some friendly advice." He then stood and stalked away. Michael shook his head. He wasn't looking forward to telling Augusta the news of South Carolina's secession. She would be worried, and rightly so. He was worried. Good people would be killed if this war, were to actually come to fruition. Michael would just have to remind himself and Augusta that they could get through anything as long as they supported each other.

Part 5: 1861

Tuesday March 12, 1861
Washington City
Dear Azalea,

I miss everyone in Charleston so! I hope this letter finds you well, even with the turmoil our statesmen have pulled our country into. I know you will agree with me that it was a foolish move for South Carolina to secede and start this whole conflict. Michael and I were lucky enough to be able to hear the President's inaugural speech last month. It was quite good in my opinion. He reminded everyone that we are not enemies, but friends, and that we must not become enemies. I completely agree with him. If only the radicals would be more tolerant and listen! Did you hear that poor Mr. Lincoln had some excitement on his way to the capital while passing through Baltimore. There were mobs of men waiting to kill him, but luckily, his personal guards were able to stop the would-be assassins. The rumor is that it was a young woman who came up with the plan to get him safely to Washington. I had to chuckle when I heard the news. Most men wouldn't think a woman could be so smart, but I say that you should never doubt the intelligence of a woman.

You asked in your last letter how Michael and I celebrated our first Christmas as a married couple. While it was enchanting to spend the holiday with my husband, we dearly missed our families and friends. However, I may be home, sooner rather than later. Once Michael's regiment moves out, I'll be on my way to Carolina. I wouldn't be able to stay here in Washington by myself, as there is much animosity towards any Southerner. I believe even Michael is taking much abuse from his colleagues in regards to his Southern wife, but he never lets on. He is such a kind-hearted man.

Oh, and such splendid news! We were finally able to see Joseph. He could only stay long enough to have dinner, as he was resigning from the Union Army. As I suspected, he will join with the new Southern army. Michael was very upset at this news. They parted amicably, but both realized the next time they see each other could be on the battlefield. It makes me sick to think of that happening.

Please give my regards to Aunt Bernice. I hope to get a letter to her soon.

Take care, my friend,
Augusta

Saturday, April 13, 1861
Washington City

Augusta was sitting at the table, writing an overdue letter to her Aunt Bernice when Michael stepped up behind her and kissed her on the head. She smiled and stood to take him in her arms.

"I didn't even hear you come in." She went to kiss him, then pulled back when she saw the expression on his face. "Michael, whatever is wrong?"

"I only stopped by for a moment, to say goodbye. I may not be back for a few days."

Augusta's heart pounded. "Whatever do you mean? What's happened?"

Michael led her to the bed and sat down. Augusta reluctantly sat next to him. "The war has officially started." He spoke quietly. Augusta gasped. She knew she shouldn't be surprised, but she had so hoped that all the controversy wouldn't lead to a war. A tear slipped down her cheek.

"Do you know where you'll be for the duration of the war?" She knew that they would soon be separated. She tried to be brave for Michael.

"I'm not sure when or where I'll be reassigned. When I get my orders, I will have to leave fairly quickly. There is a small chance that I could be assigned to Washington for a time. That would be ideal for us. When I do leave..."

"I don't want to talk about that, Michael. Not now. Not yet." She hugged him tightly. "We can worry about all that later, can't we?"

"Certainly," he replied, reluctant to discuss his leaving as well. The clock on the mantle chimed. He sighed. "I must report for a special assignment. As I said, I might not be back for a couple of days. It would be best if you stayed closer to home until I come back. It will be safer."

"Of course," Augusta said. She would hate being cooped up in the hotel room, but she didn't want to find any trouble just by venturing out around town.

Michael stood and pulled her into another hug. "I will miss you dearly," he murmured.

"And I you." Augusta kissed him. "Take care of yourself, Lieutenant Lewis. Come back to me as soon as you are able."

"I will do my best, Mrs. Lewis," he replied, then, with a final kiss, Michael went out the door.

Monday, April 15, 1861
Washington City

Michael had returned late the night before. He had been riding patrol and making sure earthenworks could be constructed and the best places to locate them in order to protect the capitol. He presently found himself in bed with Augusta, lazily stroking her arm. Michael smiled and kissed her temple. She stirred, opened her bright blue eyes and gave him a sleepy smile.

"Good morning," She turned in his arms and kissed his cheek, her blonde hair falling over her shoulder. "What are you grinning about?" She was unable to keep from smiling herself.

"Just thinking about you. The day we met. How lucky I am. Thanking the good Lord for all my blessings."

"Ah, the day we met." She snuggled into his arms. "The day that you couldn't even speak to me because you were so nervous."

"Don't tease me. You were, and still are the most beautiful woman I have ever met." He leaned back and looked at her. "All I knew about Southern women was that they were spoiled and persnickety and that they only liked the elegant, fancy men with money and property."

"So you're using that excuse again." She laughed. "Well, I find that I must thank you again for finally finding the courage to actually talk to me."

Augusta paused and thought back to the path that had taken her from her plantation home in South Carolina, to being the wife of a Northern army officer. She still wondered if her father and Andrew would ever really accept the marriage. Always able to read her expression, Michael commented about the worried look on her face.

"What are you thinking about?" Michael whispered against her ear. "Your family again?"

"Yes." She admitted. "I wish I could see them again. It's been almost a year since I have seen Andrew and my father. After seeing Joseph last week, I miss them all the more. With this war almost on our doorstep, I wonder if I'll see any of them again." Her voice turned to a whisper, her vulnerability apparent.

"I miss Joseph too. He's my best friend and I'm none too happy about his decision to go south and join the Confederacy. I do understand, I suppose. It only makes sense that he would choose to fight for his land and family," he sighed. "This blasted conflict is finally here. I knew it was inevitable, yet I hoped and prayed that the two sides would come to a compromise. The hardest thing I will have to do is leave you."

Augusta felt a tear roll down her cheek. "I hate the senselessness of it all. I can't fathom any of this. I can't understand why men are so prideful that they cannot work out their differences peacefully." She knew the time had come to finally talk to Michael of what her plans were for when he was transferred. She knew that her next sentence would cause a disagreement. "I wonder how father will act towards me when I arrive home, because I will go home, to wait for you there..." The slight hesitant look in Michael's eyes made Augusta's heart sink.

"Augusta, I have decided that you can't go home, not south anyways, not now, not until the war ends. I won't allow it." He averted his eyes, but his voice was commanding.

"Yes, I can and I will!"

"It's too dangerous. You cannot go to South Carolina."

"Yes I can and I must. What do you mean it will be too dangerous? The war's not supposed to last long, only a few months. I'll just go home to be sure everyone is alright and I will visit for a spell. When this pointless war is over and you come back home from your tour of duty, I will return. I surely can't stay here alone. This being the capitol, well, staying here would be what's dangerous. Where else am I supposed to go?"

"Augusta, listen to me, please. This war is going to last a lot longer than people realize. Neither side will give up easily. The North may have more men and many more factories for supplies and munitions, but your Southern men will be the more experienced soldiers. Combine that with the southern pride you're always talking about and they just may best us. Most of them have spent a good deal of their lives hunting and riding horses, you know that." He hesitated and continued, "I also believe that most of the battles will be fought in the southern states. The South will be fighting a defensive war; they will be fighting on land they have grown up on. The Union army will be the aggressor. I can't have you in harm's way, I just can't. Besides, even if you left tomorrow, the trip would be too dangerous and difficult. There is no one to accompany you. You would be traveling alone."

"Then what am I supposed to do, Michael? Stay here in Washington all by myself and be worried out of my mind about you and my family?" She pushed him over and stood up, then turned around and looked down at him. She was angry, and frustrated at the whole situation. She had known this time would come and that he would be leaving her. They had avoided talking about it, both hating to even think about it. But they could no longer avoid the discussion.

Sitting back up, Michael answered. "As you said, that won't be such a good idea either. Washington could be just as dangerous, it being the capital city. I have decided to send you to Gettysburg. You can stay with my mother and father. Gettysburg is a small town, you will be safe there."

Augusta blinked, and then ran her hand through her blonde waves. "Gettysburg? But I've never been there and I've only met your parents twice. I won't know anybody there."

"You'll adjust. People love you. My parents love you. You are an expert in socializing and very friendly. You'll make friends fast."

"I highly doubt that, Michael, when my family is fighting for the Confederacy? My southern accent will be frowned upon and you know it. What makes Gettysburg any different than Washington? I don't think I'll be making any friends at all."

"They're good people in Gettysburg, Augusta. As I said, my parents love you. Trust me." He leaned over and kissed the tear on her cheek. "I know it will be difficult." He spoke in a soft voice. "We knew this day would come."

"I know." She reached up and wove her hands through his hair. "I'm not mad because you want me to go to Gettysburg. I hadn't even thought of that. I would rather just go home. I miss my family. I understand why you don't want me to. It's more ...I don't want to leave you. When you go...I just don't know how I'll say goodbye. What if...what if you don't come back?" The last sentence was spoken so softly, he almost missed it.

"I'll have God with me. He'll watch over the both of us. I'll visit you if I ever get the chance and I'll write frequently. We will get through this, Augusta. I can't promise that I'll come back alive; I won't make a promise like that, but one way or another, we'll see each other again."

Augusta sighed "If and when you do get transferred, I will agree to go to your parents," She finally conceded. "I will just hope and pray you are assigned to a safe city where I can accompany you."

Tuesday, June 11, 1861
Washington City

My Dear Azalea,

This very well may be the last letter you receive from me coming from Washington City. My luggage has been sent ahead, and today I will board a train and head north to Gettysburg. Michael believes it is a quiet enough town and will not be disturbed by any battles that are sure to come. In fact, the Confederates are moving toward the Union capital as we speak, if intelligence is to be believed. How did we come to this?

I know it will only be a matter of time before Andrew joins Joseph in the Confederate army, and Father may sign up as well. I am truly afraid of this war for so many reasons, but one of them is knowing that South Carolina started it and so may be hit the hardest. Many here in Washington are confident of a quick northern victory, but if I know Southerners and their determination, they are feeling the same confidence.

I wish I could follow Michael, wherever he is sent. Some women follow their husbands. Michael wants to keep me safe, though. He assures me that his parents are very excited to have me stay with them, but I must confess I am nervous that they will not like me. Please keep me in your thoughts and prayers regarding this.

I'm not even sure if this letter will reach you. According to the politicians, we now live in two different countries! It is so difficult to believe. I will constantly be worried for you and all my family and friends. I cannot imagine that it has come to this.

As always, give Aunt Bernice my love when you see her, and please stay out of harm's way. I miss you dearly. I hope that when this madness is over, we can have a nice long visit.

Your friend,

Augusta

Train Station

Augusta tried to be strong, tried to hold her emotions in check. The day she had prayed would never come was here. Michael would be moving to a camp south of Washington, and she was boarding a train to Pennsylvania. She knew in her heart that Michael's parents would treat her kindly, probably like their own daughter, but she was still extremely wary. The prejudice she had faced in Washington had been bearable because Michael had been at her side. How would she survive being further north while separated from her husband?

"I don't want to say goodbye," she whispered, though she knew he didn't want to either. "Are you positive I can't travel with you? Where you go, I will go..."

"I can't have you that close to the danger, Augusta. You know that. An army camp is no place for a lady. I wouldn't want you exposed to the everyday life of a soldier, especially the diseases and vermin found there." Michael hadn't told her about Lieutenant Mason's comments, and didn't intend to now. The man hadn't relented in his despicable comments, and Michael was glad to have Augusta away from the city where the cad would remain stationed. "Remember the rest of the verse?"

"Your people will be my people..."

"Yes. My parents are excited to have you. They'll take care of you. I would trust no one to watch over you as well as them."

"I know you're right. Truly, I do." Augusta wiped a tear from her cheek.

"Augusta, I don't know when or if I will see you again."

"Michael, please don't say that." Augusta shook her head.

"No, Augusta, I must. Please let me get through this." He took his hat off. "Augusta, if I don't come back, you must get on with your life. Don't be afraid to fall in love again."

"Michael, please I don't want to think about this."

"I know. I don't either, but I need you to know that if something does happen, don't mourn overlong. And please, don't blame God."

"I understand you need to tell me this, but thanks to you, I have faith that you will make it home alive. If, God forbid, you don't make it home, I'll lean on the fact that we will be together Heaven."

The train whistled and chugged into the station. Augusta's heart raced. As much as she prayed it wasn't so, this could be the last time she would ever see Michael. She threw herself into his arms.

"Write me as often as you can," she whispered. He brushed a kiss on her cheek and she leaned into his shoulder.

"I will. And I look forward to the letters I will receive from you."

"Every week." Augusta pulled back. "And when this war is over, I will never let you out of my sight again."

The train whistled again and the conductor began his call: "All Aboard!"

"And when this war is over, I will not let you out of my sight, you can follow me wherever I go." Michael whispered against her cheek.

"You know I will."

Michael led her to the last train car, then pulled her close for one final kiss. "I love you, Augusta."

She hugged him tightly. "I love you too, always and forever." Reluctantly, Augusta boarded the train, a small carpet bag in hand. As the train pulled away from the station, she stood on the platform on the back of the train and continued to watch Michael.

She brushed a single tear from her cheek and took a deep breath to fortify herself. Her heart felt like it was being torn in two, but she knew deep down that with the love of her family and friends from both north and south, and her growing faith in God, that she and Michael could get through anything. Augusta waved one last time and then Michael was gone from her sight.

Images

Rose O'Neill
Greenhow

Charleston, South Carolina

West Point Cadets

Harper's Ferry, Virginia

Fort Sumter, Charleston Harbor

The US Capitol Building, 1860

Author's Note

I have always had a love of history especially the time period of the American Civil War. To me, history isn't just famous people, events and dates. It is the stories of those everyday normal citizens who are caught in the middle of the conflict through no fault of their own and must struggle through the times as best they can. It always fascinates me how they were able to survive and persevere.

Thank you so much for reading the prequel novella *Wherever You* Go. I enjoyed writing it very much and I hope you enjoyed reading about Michael and Augusta and how their relationship developed. While this novella is fiction, it is an introduction to my historically accurate 'Turner Daughters' series novels. Augusta and Michael's story is continued in *Though War Shall Rise Against Me*, the first novel in the series. You will not only learn more about Augusta and Michael, you will also read about the civilians of Gettysburg, Pennsylvania during the Civil War, including Charlotte Turner, the daughter of a local farmer, newlywed Alexandria Sadler, and seamstress Ginny Wade (a true civilian that lived in Gettysburg during the Civil War). They must all come together to support one another during this turbulent time in our history.

Though War Shall Rise Against Me and all of my novels are available on Amazon or by e-mailing me at ericamarie84@gmail.com.

About the Author

Erica "Marie LaPres" Emelander is a middle school social studies and religion teacher who lives in Grand Rapids, Michigan. Erica has always enjoyed reading and writing. Combine that with her love of history and God, you will see that she has incorporated all four loves into her novels. Erica has written three novels in the Turner Daughter series. She also has a Middle Grade novel, Whom Shall I Fear: Sammy's Struggle, and a Young Adult Novel. Beyond the Fort. She also writes a monthly article on Michigan history for 'Buy Now Michigan'. When not working on and researching her books, Erica can be found coaching middle and high school sports, being a youth minister, and spending time with her friends and family, especially her beloved nieces and nephews.

Find Erica on:
Email: ericamarie84@gmail.com
Facebook: "Marie LaPres"
GoodReads: Marie LaPres
Instagram: marielapres
Blogger: authormarielapres

Other books by Marie LaPres

The Turner Daughter Series

The War Between the States has finally come and the civilians of Gettysburg hope the battles will stay as far away from them as possible. But the war will touch them all more than they can imagine. Four friends, old and new, will find themselves looking to God and each other to get them through.

Kate, America Joan, and sisters Belle and Elizabeth enjoy their lives in the safe, "finished" town of Fredericksburg, Virginia. Then, the Civil War breaks out and their lives will never be the same. Will the Civil War affect the women and their town? Will they lose faith, or always remain 'Strong and Steadfast'?

The citizens of Vicksburg never wanted secession, much less a war, but when Mississippi secedes from the United States, they throw their support behind the Confederacy. They hope the battles will stay far away from their bustling trade center, but they realize the importance of their town, perfectly situated atop a hill at a bend on the mighty Mississippi River. Then the siege comes…

Young Adult Novel: Key to Mackinaw Series

Christine Belanger has always loved learning about the past, but she may get more history than she bargained for when she finds herself at Colonial Michilimackinac in the year 1775. When the tensions between the French and the British reach a tipping point, it falls to Christine and fellow time traveler Henri to save the settlers, and possibly change the course of history. Can Christine and Henri outwit Lewis and save the fort? Will Christine be able to survive Colonial America without all of the amenities she is used to...especially her cell phone?

Middle Grade Novel: Whom Shall I Fear: Sammy's Struggle

Twelve-year-old Samuel Wade's life has never been easy, but the coming of the American Civil War makes it even more difficult. Then the war comes to his hometown of Gettysburg and he must make quick decisions that could mean life or death. Will Samuel be able to keep Emma out of harms way? Will he be able to watch over his family? Will he finally be able to earn the respect of the townspeople who look down on him?